Flashback

SIMON ROSE

Flashback

SIMON ROSE

TYCHE BOOKS LTD.

Flashback
Published by Tyche Books Ltd.
www.TycheBooks.com

Copyright © 2015 Simon Rose
First Tyche Books Ltd Edition 2015

Print ISBN: 978-1-928025-11-5
Ebook ISBN: 978-1-928025-23-8

Cover Art by Artist Wiktoria Goc
Cover Layout by Lucia Starkey
Interior Layout by Ryah Deines
Editorial by M. L. D. Curelas

Author photograph: Simon Rose

Alberta
Government

This book was funded in part by a grant from the Alberta Media Fund.

Dedication

"Escape into your imagination and always dare to dream."

This book is dedicated to my family, a rock and an anchor in ever changing times.

Contents

CHAPTER ONE
FLASHBACKS

"ARE THE RESTRAINTS tight enough?"

"Yes, of course they are. I told you, I know what I'm doing."

"Now keep still, David, this won't hurt a bit."

The twisted smile on the doctor's face told a far different story. Max struggled against the bonds securing him to the operating table as the old man's hand moved closer. Max clearly saw the hypodermic, the needle now only inches from his eye. The younger man with the long blonde hair and pale blue eyes grinned, as Max emitted a scream that he was certain no one would ever hear.

"You okay, Max?" Jeff asked. "You don't look so good."

Max felt dizzy and disoriented, having to rest his hand on the taller headstone to steady himself.

Max and Jeff had gone to grab some pizza that afternoon. It was the start of summer vacation and Jeff had to stop and buy some flowers then meet his grandmother at Queen's Park Cemetery. Jeff's grandfather had passed away about six weeks earlier and his grandmother still liked to go to pay her respects and freshen the flowers beside the grave.

The boys had just been chatting to Mrs. McNally and Max had stepped away to give the two family members a few moments of privacy. He was standing by a tall elaborate headstone mounted on a marble pedestal, belonging to someone called Jonathan Dexter. There was a smaller headstone beside the pedestal. Before Max could read the name, his hand brushed the edge of the smaller gravestone. Disconnected, random images had suddenly flashed across his mind, culminating in the terrifying scene with the needle.

"I don't feel so good either," admitted Max, running his fingers through his light brown hair and rubbing the back of his neck.

"Did you hit your head or something?" Jeff asked.

"I don't think so," replied Max, "but now I have this splitting headache."

"Are you sure you're okay, Max?" asked Mrs. McNally, with an expression of concern.

"Yeah, I think so," said Max, forcing a smile, although his head was truly pounding, and it must have shown in his face.

"You going to be okay for the game?" Jeff asked. "You've never missed one yet."

Max had almost forgotten that he was playing third base that afternoon. Yet he knew he couldn't play, feeling the way he did, even if he was reluctant to let Jeff know that.

"You certainly do look a little pale, Max," remarked Mrs. McNally.

"Maybe you should just go home?" Jeff suggested. "I'll get someone to fill in on third, no big deal."

"You might be right," said Max. "Sorry about the game."

"No problem," said Jeff. "Jason and the others will be there. Are you sure you're going to be okay?"

"Yeah," Max nodded. "You'd better get going or you'll miss everyone."

"Well, we're about done here," said Mrs. McNally. "You go with Max, Jeff. Uncle Bill said he'd be here at 1.30 to take me home anyway."

"You sure, Grandma?"

"Yes, I'm sure," replied Mrs. McNally. "You go ahead."

Jeff gave his grandmother a peck on the cheek and he and Max made their way out of the cemetery.

They waited for the lights to change at the nearby intersection. Sitting on the bench beside the bus stop was a boy around their own age in a black tee shirt and jeans, with a thick mop of dark hair almost completely covering his eyes. He was staring right at them. Although Max was sure he'd never seen the boy before, at school or anywhere else, he looked oddly familiar.

"Is he from school?" he asked Jeff.

"Huh?"

"That kid?"

"What?"

"Over there, on the bench," said Max, just as the lights changed.

"What?" Jeff repeated, as they set off across the road.

When Max looked again, the bench was empty. The boy must have gone, but as Max scanned the area, there was no sign of him. A bus hadn't driven by and there was no way the boy could have gotten away that quickly. Max knew he'd seen someone, but kept his thoughts to himself. He rubbed the back of his neck again.

"You okay?" asked Jeff when they reached the other side of the road.

"Yeah," Max assured him, "just that headache."

"So," said Jeff, as they arrived at the corner of the street where Max lived, "still on for this weekend at Jason's?"

"Hope so," said Max. "I've been dying to play Jason's new game all week."

"Me too," Jeff agreed.

He started off down the sidewalk to walk the couple of blocks to his own house.

"Hey, sorry about this afternoon," Max called after him.

"No problem," Jeff assured him. "Like I said, I'll get somebody to cover third. I'll text you tonight."

As he turned his key in the lock, Max could still vividly recall the strange visions that had flooded across his mind when he'd touched the gravestone. A smiling woman walking into a room carrying a cake decorated with fourteen lighted candles; piles of wrapped gifts surrounding a huge Christmas tree; sailing on the ocean aboard a luxurious yacht; skiing at an alpine resort; a musical concert at a theatre; a

4

shiny black limousine; a dinner party in a luxurious ballroom; and finally, the scientific facility with men and women in white lab coats, including the horrifying image of the needle.

His headache had subsided, but when he opened the door to the condo, Max's headache returned as he was greeted by the screech of a power saw. His dad was still working in the basement.

Max closed the front door and headed downstairs. His dad had been busy on the renovations in the basement for months, but had now almost finished. He worked as a carpenter in the local construction industry, but despite the fact that somebody always seemed to be building something new, his dad's fortunes fluctuated. Sometimes, Max hardly saw his father for weeks at a time. When work was plentiful, his dad left early in the morning and returned home well after dark. At other times, like recently, jobs had been scarce and his dad had filled his time working on the renovations. Such a lifestyle hardly helped their financial stability as a family. His dad had been promising Max that they'd move to a bigger place and in a different part of town. Yet they'd been living in the same cramped condo for several years now.

When he reached the bottom of the basement steps, all the dust in the air made Max cough and splutter.

"Hey Max," said his dad, as he turned off the saw. "What's up?"

"Nothing much," Max replied, with a shrug, as he sat down on an upturned toolbox. "Just out with Jeff. Dad, who was Jonathan Dexter?"

"The Dexters?" said his dad. "They were a very prominent local family once. Jonathan Dexter was an important politician. Even talked about as a potential president, I think. Why do you ask?"

"Jeff had to meet his grandma at the cemetery on the way home and I saw the big headstone, that's all," Max explained. "There was another grave next to Dexter's, but I didn't see the name."

"Probably belongs to Dexter's son, David," said his dad. "He disappeared when he was about your age. He was a brilliant student and a virtuoso pianist, wonderful prospects. Tragic really."

"Why?" Max asked. "What happened?"

"A few years ago," his dad continued, "they found a skeleton in a remote area west of the city and identified it as David's. It was in all the papers. Not long afterwards, Jonathan Dexter himself died and they built that fancy grave. Why are you so interested in this all of a sudden?"

"No reason really," said Max, standing up. "I just wondered who he was."

"So are you here to help me with this drywall?"

"Love to, Dad," said Max, grinning, "but I've got things to do."

"Like what?"

"Just stuff," replied Max, as he climbed the stairs.

When he reached the top, Max glanced over at the pictures of his mother on the shelf above the fireplace. There were several photographs of a strikingly beautiful woman in her mid-twenties, with shoulder-length, light brown hair and hazel eyes. Max's mother had died just after he was born, so he'd never known her. Thinking back to the huge memorial to Jonathan Dexter or the more modest gravesite Jeff's grandmother had been tending, Max was struck by the fact that his mother had never had a grave for him to visit. She'd been cremated and Max's dad always insisted that he didn't need a fancy tombstone to remember her.

Max went up to his room, which as usual resembled a scene in the aftermath of a small hurricane. Twisted bedclothes lay where Max had left them when he'd tumbled out of bed that morning, alongside random items of clothing. The desk was covered in papers, binders, and folders, while two empty pop cans and half a bag of chips stood next to a book lying spine up that Max hadn't touched for months. The shelves on the wall were filled with other books that Max had often started but never managed to finish. There was also a collection of medals and figurines he'd received in previous years along with the other members of his soccer and baseball teams. A selection of well-thumbed comic books lay next to the lamp on the bedside table. Most of his friends no longer read comics, but Max had been a fan since he was six or seven years old and still enjoyed them.

Max's game system, accompanied by a bewildering tangle of wires and cables, sat beside a small TV on top of the three-drawer dresser. Empty game cases and loose discs were scattered around, a reminder of the sleepover with Jeff and two of his other friends the previous weekend. Max sat down on the bed and reached for the remote, when he suddenly felt really cold, just for a second. Max glanced at the window. It wasn't open, and even if it had been, it was a really warm day outside. Max was about to turn on the TV when everything went black.

In a scientific facility, a female patient, who had

short-cropped, green hair, was restrained on a table for some kind of medical procedure, but was still struggling. A woman in a white lab coat injected something into the patient's lower arm, and the young woman soon lay quiet. A circular device was placed over her head and a screen behind the operating table became illuminated. Swirling shapes flickered across the surface of the screen, but before Max could make them out clearly, everything shifted yet again.

"Are the restraints tight enough?"

"Yes, of course they are. I told you, I know what I'm doing."

"Now keep still, David, this won't hurt a bit."

Max struggled against the bonds securing him to the operating table. The hypodermic needle in the doctor's hand was now only inches away from Max's eye. The younger man with the long hair and pale blue eyes grinned. Max screamed and abruptly woke up in his own bedroom, gasping for breath.

He sat up on the bed, clutching at his chest, his heart still pounding. Max gradually began to compose himself and breathe normally, but his mind was still racing. The images that had flooded into his mind at the cemetery had returned and this time they'd seemed so real.

Max knew that he couldn't mention anything to his dad, who was certain to mention Dr. Hammond. Max was determined to avoid another round of sessions with a shrink to discuss odd dreams and potential mental health issues. There just had to be some other explanation for the strange mental images he'd experienced.

Max knew that he had to find out more, so he went

downstairs. Standing at the top of the steps leading to the basement, Max called down to his dad.

"Can I use the computer yet?"

"Sorry," his dad apologized, "not yet. I had to unplug everything in the office to access the wiring in the wall."

Max cursed under his breath. He hated being reminded of the fact that he was probably the only kid in school who didn't even have a desktop computer of his own. And his laptop had been getting fixed at the store for weeks now. Fortunately his dad hardly ever used the computer and didn't really know PDF from ABC. He could barely deal with e-mail, so it wasn't as if Max had any real competition to get online.

"I think I'll go down to the library and get on a computer there," he announced.

"Okay," his dad acknowledged. "I'll probably be out when you get back, but there should be something to eat in the fridge."

"Great," said Max. "See you later."

Max had to wait patiently before he could ride his bike across the busy intersection where the library was located. When the lights changed, Max hurried across the road and headed toward the library's front entrance, securing his bike in the rack. Once inside, he immediately saw that only one of the computers was unoccupied. Max went over and sat down, next to an old man with a gray goatee and wearing a blue baseball cap. Max then quickly keyed in his library card number and logged on to the Internet.

Max wasn't entirely sure what he was looking for, except that he wanted to learn more about the Dexter family, so he Googled "Jonathan Dexter". He'd been a very important politician, so there were numerous sites containing information about him and his family. Throughout his career, Jonathan Dexter had worked in several different government agencies, mainly concerned with science and research and almost all connected to the military. One website had a collection of photographs of Dexter with a group of high ranking army officers, plus men and women wearing white lab coats taken at some kind of unnamed scientific facility.

As Max's dad had explained earlier, Dexter had once been considered as a possible presidential candidate. He'd been a high flyer and had been respected on both sides of the political divide, even by his fiercest opponents. However, although Dexter had seemed to be ready to resume his career following a brief pause after his son's disappearance, he unexpectedly didn't stand for reelection and announced his retirement from politics. He later emerged as a champion of several charities and groups dedicated to finding missing children, until his death.

Clicking on another link, Max read Jonathan Dexter's obituary. He'd died as the result of a fire at his home and while there was only a brief mention of Dexter's wife, there were several references to his son. Max eagerly moved on to the web pages related to the disappearance of David Dexter.

At the time, David's parents were featured in several TV appeals concerning the whereabouts of their son. Jonathan Dexter's status in the public eye had kept the case active and in the newspapers for months, but eventually the search was called off.

David had been academically brilliant, from one of the city's most prominent families, and appeared to have a great future. He'd been fourteen when he disappeared. The picture of him had been taken at some kind of musical event.

David was never found and was widely presumed to be dead. Then a few years later, the discovery of David's remains buried in a forest west of the city caused a sensation. The Dexter case was suddenly in the news again, just prior to Jonathan Dexter's own death. However, what really caught Max's attention was that the police had apparently received a tip from a local psychic regarding the location of the body.

Max was eager to do further research but the library was getting ready to close for the day. Disappointed, he left the library and headed for the bike rack.

CHAPTER TWO
THE OLD MAN

MAX DIDN'T GO straight home. There was a coffee shop nearby where he could get a cool drink resembling his favourite iced cappuccino. Max leaned his bike up against the railing outside the coffee shop and went inside. He ordered his drink and went outside to sit at one of the patio tables. Max took out his cellphone and opened one of his games. He was so engrossed that he scarcely noticed when a bespectacled old man with a gray goatee wearing a blue baseball cap came around the corner. The man wrapped his small black dog's leash around the railing where Max had leaned his bike.

"Excuse me."

"Huh?"

"Would you mind just watching my dog for a minute, while I grab a coffee?" asked the old man.

"He's very well behaved."

"Yeah, whatever," said Max, seeing no harm in it.

A few minutes later, the old man returned with a coffee and a small cookie, much to the dog's delight.

"Thanks a lot," said the old man.

He sat down and tossed a piece of the cookie to his dog.

"I told you he'd be no trouble. Sure is a nice evening."

Max paid no attention and remained focused on his cellphone.

"So why were you looking into the Dexter case?" said the old man.

"What?" Max asked, turning to stare at the stranger beside him.

"I was on the computer beside you at the library," the man explained. "Why are you so interested in David Dexter?"

"I've got to do a summer project for school about old newspaper stories," Max lied. "I found those articles by accident."

"It was quite a story back then," said the old man, taking a sip from his coffee, "before they just buried the case. Too many secrets, I guess."

"Is that right?" said Max, disinterestedly, returning his attention to his game.

"John Carrington," the old man said, handing Max a business card.

"A private investigator?" said Max skeptically, as he took the card and quickly scanned the words.

"Sort of," replied Carrington. "I rarely take on any jobs now. Back then I was working with the city police, investigating David Dexter's disappearance. That is, until I was taken off the case."

"Oh yeah," Max said, as he finished his drink.

He stood up from the table and put his cellphone in his pocket.

"Well, I'd better get moving," said Max, handing Carrington the business card.

"Hey, keep the card, kid," Carrington told him. "If you want to know any more about the Dexter case for that school project, I'm usually in Castlegate Park around noon. We sit on the benches over by the lake."

"Okay," said Max, stuffing the card into his pocket and grabbing his bike. "Bye."

As Max pushed the bike around the corner of the coffee shop, a white car pulled into one of the parking spaces. Two men wearing dark suits got out of the car's front seats. One was tall and willowy with thinning, pale blonde hair. The other was shorter and more heavily built, dark haired with a gray peppered goatee. A third man, with longer, blonde hair, was just getting out of the back seat when he got a call on his cell phone.

"What do you want anyway?" asked the man with the goatee.

"Americano, large, room for cream," replied the third man as he leaned on the car's open back door. "I have to take this call from the station. I'll see you guys in a minute."

The first two men brushed past Max and went into the coffee shop's side entrance. Max was about to get on his bike and ride away when he noticed a boy outside the bank on the far side of the parking lot. It looked like the same boy Max had seen at the bus stop when he and Jeff had been walking home from the cemetery. Dressed in a black tee shirt and

15

jeans, with thick dark hair, the boy just stood there, looking over at Max. The boy then started to walk across the parking lot toward him, but Max was startled when his bike clattered to the ground. The man who'd been in the back seat of the white car had dropped his cell phone as he and Max had collided.

"Hey, watch where you're going," he snarled, as he picked up his phone from the sidewalk and dusted it off. "Damn, I've lost the call."

"Sorry," said Max.

"Yeah, you should be," said the man, angrily, but then his expression changed and he looked at Max curiously. "Do I know you?"

Max noticed that the man's eyes were a very pale, piercing blue.

"Don't think so," said Max, although for a fleeting moment he thought the man looked oddly familiar somehow.

"Okay, well like I said, just watch it, kid."

The man hurried to join his colleagues inside the coffee shop. Glancing around the parking lot, Max saw no sign of the boy in the black tee shirt. He climbed onto his bike and rode away.

It was almost nine when Max got home. He fastened the bike to the pipe near the gas meter and went inside the condo. His dad was still out and hadn't given Max any indication of when he might be back. Max checked in the fridge, where he found his dad had left some of the stew from the previous evening for him. Max took the bowl out of the fridge, put it in the microwave, and set the timer. While he was waiting, he turned on the TV. Despite the fact that they could access over a hundred channels, there really wasn't much to choose from.

When the microwave had finished, he turned off the TV and went to eat his stew in the kitchen. While he was eating, Max thought about the old man he'd met at the coffee shop. Could he really have worked on the Dexter case and was he really a private detective? He'd produced a business card, but Max was well aware that Carrington could easily have had those printed just about anywhere.

Still, it was all quite intriguing and the old man seemed safe enough. Max was interested in finding out more about David Dexter. He saw no harm in taking Carrington up on his invitation to meet at the park the next day. Max finished his stew and put his bowl and spoon in the dishwasher. He contemplated watching some TV after all, but could hardly keep his eyes open. It was only just before ten o'clock and Max had no idea why he was so tired. What's more, his headache appeared to be coming back. Figuring that an early night may do him some good, Max went upstairs and was asleep moments after his head hit the pillow.

CHAPTER THREE
TELLING STORIES

MAX DIDN'T WAKE up until eleven o'clock the next morning. He was still a little groggy as he clambered out of bed, but took a quick shower and went downstairs. A glance outside told Max that the truck was missing. His dad wasn't around, but he did sometimes go out to buy renovation supplies.

Max's headache had gone and he hadn't had any dreams—or at least none that he could remember. Yet he still vividly recalled the images that had flashed across his mind at the cemetery, plus the terrifying vision of the man with the needle.

All of this had started after he'd touched the gravestone. Max had no idea what the connection was, but he figured he'd found out as much as he could from websites. Carrington did seem to know a lot about the Dexter family, so Max set off for

Castlegate Park.

When the bus arrived, Max climbed the steps and paid his fare. The bus was empty and Max settled into a seat at the back. When the bus slowed down as it approached a set of traffic lights, Max stared out the window and yawned. Why was he so tired? As the bus pulled away again, Max dozed off.

The white lights twinkled on the huge tree, under which lay a large number of boxes and parcels in a variety of shapes and sizes. The woman with deep chestnut brown hair cascading over her shoulders smiled at him. She handed him a gift, wrapped in bright red paper, from under the tree.

"Merry Christmas, David," she said.

"Hey, didn't you want Castlegate Park?"

Max woke up to the sound of the driver's voice. The bus had stopped beside the park. In the seat across the aisle, beside the window, sat a boy in a black tee shirt and jeans, with a thick mop of dark hair almost covering his eyes.

"Excuse me," said Max, "but do I know you?"

"No, we've never met," said the boy.

"Are you sure?" Max pressed him. "I've been to a lot of different schools and you look very familiar."

"Isn't this your stop?" said the boy.

"Yeah, it is," said Max, "but I'm certain I've seen you before."

"You must have me mixed up with someone else." The boy turned away to face the window.

"But I—" Max began.

"Hey," shouted the driver, "are you getting off

here or what?"

"Yeah," Max called back, "I'm coming."

He stood up from his seat and walked to the front of the bus. At the top of the steps, Max looked back to where he'd been sitting, but the boy was gone.

"What the . . ." he started to say.

"Are you okay?" said the driver, with a frown.

"Yeah," Max replied haltingly. "Yeah, I'm fine."

But he certainly wasn't fine. As he watched the empty bus pull away, Max knew that something was desperately wrong. He couldn't talk to anyone about it, not his friends and certainly not his dad. He certainly wasn't going to confide in the old man. Yet, Max reminded himself, his strange visions had started after he'd been in the cemetery. Maybe chatting with Carrington, who seemed to know something about the Dexter family, might be able to provide some clues as to what the hell was happening.

Max wasn't that familiar with Castlegate Park, although it wasn't that far from where he lived. He remembered going to the outdoor wading pool a few times with his dad when he was very small, but that was about it.

There were plenty of people at the park that day. Men and women taking advantage of a beautiful sunny day ate their lunches on the park benches. Joggers overtook young mothers pushing strollers along the pathway. The wading pool was particularly busy and nearby, children chased each other noisily around the brightly painted playground.

Max was wondering if he'd be able to find Carrington when he saw a small black dog relaxing on the grass beside a bench under one of the park's taller trees. Max adjusted his phone to turn off the ringer as he walked over to the bench.

"Hi, I wasn't sure whether you'd come or not," said Carrington, reaching down to calm his dog. "It's okay, Doogie, he's a friend."

"Hi," said Max, petting the dog as it licked his hand.

"So how's that project?" Carrington asked.

"What?"

"The school project, about old newspaper stories," said Carrington.

"Oh, right," Max replied.

He'd forgotten what he'd told Carrington the day before about his reason for looking into the Dexter family.

"It's coming along," he said. "I'm using the Dexter story, but I thought more research might be good."

"I certainly know something about it, depends how much you'd like to know. What's your name, by the way?"

"Max."

He sat down on the other end of the bench and the dog settled back down beside Carrington. The park was full of people, so Max thought his surroundings were pretty secure.

"Well," he began, "I read about the case online at the library and know about his dad and the politics and everything."

"Yeah," said Carrington, "David Dexter's dad was pretty well known, so it was in all the papers. I started out in the city police, but I was a private detective back then. I had a lot of experience in missing person cases, so they brought me in to help.

I uncovered what I thought was a connection to a lot of other similar cases. I thought we were getting somewhere, but they suddenly shut the whole investigation down. They eventually found David's remains in the woods, as you probably know, but I was never convinced it was such a simple case. There was a lot more to it than met the eye."

"Like what?" Max asked.

"Just things that didn't add up," replied Carrington. "Dexter resigned from politics not long after. It was officially because of the trauma of David's disappearance, but I always thought that wasn't the only reason. Then of course there was David's mother."

"What about her?" said Max, not recalling anything specific about Mrs. Dexter from his own research.

"Poor Vanessa Dexter was confined to an asylum," replied Carrington.

"An asylum?" said Max, shocked. "What for?"

"Driven 'mad with grief' after losing her son, I think was the official explanation. She's been in and out of hospitals ever since but she's in a nursing home now called Belvedere Mansions."

"I didn't know that," Max admitted.

"Again, it just seemed so unlikely to me. I met her once, just after her son disappeared and she seemed like one of the people least likely to go off the rails. I mean yes, it was a traumatic experience and who knows what went through her mind, but it just didn't ring true. Then of course, look what happened to Jonathan Dexter."

"Didn't he die in a fire?"

"So they say," said Carrington. "One afternoon,

years after David's disappearance, I received a message that Jonathan Dexter was trying to contact me with some important information."

"What was it?" said Max.

"I never found out," Carrington admitted. "The next day, Dexter was dead. I was there at the house with the police the day after the fire. The wall safe had been forced open, but the valuables were left behind. It was very suspicious. I think maybe some documents were the only things taken. Yeah, there are still a lot of questions about that whole Dexter business. So, do you think you'll be able to use some of this stuff in your school project?"

"Maybe," said Max.

For the most part, he'd listened to Carrington, trying to work out whether the old guy was really on the level. It did seem as if Carrington had actually worked on the case and was very well informed. Admittedly, he could also just have read a lot about it and formed his own crazy theories. But so far, Max hadn't heard anything that helped him understand more about his own recent bizarre experiences.

"If you're really interested in the case," said Carrington, "maybe you'd like to help me? I've been looking into these things for years, trying to get to the truth. The police aren't interested anymore and there are still probably people who'd kill to keep it all quiet."

Max gasped. "What did you say?"

"Just kidding, Max," said Carrington, with a smile. "So, what do you say? I'm here most afternoons with Doogie. We could chat some more another day, whenever you've got time? I have to go shopping for a new computer in the morning, but I should be here again just after lunch. I could even bring some papers and pictures about the case from the office for you to take a look at?"

"Why me?" said Max. "We don't even know each other."

Carrington took a tissue from his pocket, then removed his glasses and quickly cleaned them.

"I don't have long to live," Carrington explained. "I've been told my heart could stop at any time. All this will die with me."

"Sorry to hear that," said Max.

"That's not all," Carrington continued, as he replaced his glasses. "I had a dream the other night. I can't exactly recall every detail, but I remember a voice telling me to go to the library yesterday evening. It told me I'd see someone looking into the Dexter case, someone who would help put things right."

Max almost froze in his seat on the bench. Now someone else was having weird dreams about the Dexter family?

"Are you okay?" Carrington asked.

"Look, I really have to go," Max told him.

Carrington's dog started to get excited, but this time Max ignored him.

"Yeah, I, look, I'm sorry," he said. "I really have to go."

Max hurried away and didn't look back. If Carrington said anything else, Max didn't hear him. As he neared the wading pool he broke into a run, not stopping until he reached the bus stop. Catching his breath, Max was relieved to see a bus approaching. He climbed aboard and took a seat as close to the driver as he could. His mind was racing.

Max couldn't make sense of any of it and kept going over the same things again and again. He hardly noticed as he entered his own neighbourhood and nearly missed his stop.

It was still a beautiful warm afternoon, but when Max reached the front door of the condo, a shiver ran down his spine. He put the key in the lock and opened the door. He went straight to the kitchen, grabbed a couple of pieces of cold pizza from the fridge, flopped down on the couch and clicked on the TV.

Aimlessly surfing through the channels, nothing really grabbed his attention. He eventually settled on a rerun of a sitcom episode he'd seen countless times before. Yet Max wasn't really paying attention to what was happening on the screen. He couldn't stop thinking about his conversation with John Carrington at the park. The guy had seemed nice enough at first and was probably harmless. But Max also knew that he could also just be another wacko, wandering around the park looking for someone to talk to about his wild stories. Max had no intention of meeting Carrington again. He had no doubt that the old man would subject some other poor unsuspecting passerby to his ramblings the following day.

Eventually, Max's eyelids grew heavy. It was only mid-afternoon, but for some reason he was utterly exhausted. He yawned as the sitcom's credits rolled, before making his way upstairs. He took his cell phone out of his pocket to turn it off for the night. There was a text message from Jeff, asking how Max was feeling. Another text from Jason asked Max if he was coming over on Saturday night. Max was going to reply, but could barely keep his eyes open. He turned off the phone and placed it on the desk. Resolving to message his friends in the morning, Max got undressed and climbed into bed. Minutes later he was sound asleep.

If Max had any dreams overnight, he couldn't remember them when he awoke the next day. He switched on his phone, noting the messages from Jeff and Jason, and told himself he'd reply to them while he ate breakfast. However, when Max headed downstairs and picked up the newspaper lying on the porch, he immediately noticed the headline above a short article at the edge of the front page.

Man Found Dead in Castlegate Park.

CHAPTER FOUR
PRIVATE INVESTIGATIONS

AT THE KITCHEN table, Max read the newspaper story four times.

A body found last night in Castlegate Park has been identified as John Carrington, aged sixty four. The cause of death has not been officially released, but police have ruled out foul play. It is suspected that Mr. Carrington had a heart attack and fell into the wading pool, where he was found face down by a jogger just after ten thirty. Mr. Carrington was a former employee of the city police, who also worked for a number of years as a private detective.

There was a photograph of Carrington, taken years earlier, yet Max clearly recognized the man he'd so recently spoken to at the park. Max remembered how Carrington had told him that he didn't have long to live, but it seemed so tragic that he'd just drop dead like that. And so soon after Max had talked to him. The old man had indicated that there were still a lot of unanswered questions about the Dexter case. He'd joked about people being prepared to kill to keep things quiet, but now Max wondered if there had been a grain of truth in that. And if Carrington had been murdered, someone might have seen Max talking to him at the park.

He desperately needed time to think. A sound from upstairs told Max that his dad was out of bed and would soon be coming down for breakfast. Max put the newspaper to one side and hurried out the door. At the end of the street, he fumbled in his pocket, pulling out a handful of coins, amounting to a few dollars, and Carrington's business card. The old man had mentioned that he was willing to show Max some material about the Dexter case. Max memorized Carrington's office address. Shoving the business card back into his pocket, Max hurried to the nearest bus stop.

It took Max about twenty minutes to reach the office, located in a single story commercial building not far from the coffee shop where he and Carrington had first met. There were only a few cars in the parking lot since it was Saturday. A van from a plumbing company and a pickup truck belonging to a construction firm were parked outside the front doors. On the wall inside the building's front entrance was a plaque listing the building's tenants. Suite 111 belonged to "John Carrington, Private

Investigator".

An insurance agent and a financial consultant were open for business, but otherwise the building was quiet. Max saw men tearing up carpet and replacing lights and wiring in one suite, and doing some work on the plumbing and heating systems in another. The fact that there were people working in some of the offices made Max appear a little less conspicuous as he wandered around. Even the woman who was vacuuming the hallway didn't give Max a second glance.

When he reached Carrington's office, Max was pleasantly surprised to find the door slightly ajar. There was a thick cable stretching out across the hallway and Max figured someone was working inside. He gently eased the door open, but the office was empty. Max counted eight medium-sized filing cabinets, some with the drawers still open, others with stacks of papers piled on top of them. Just inside the front door, a solitary winter coat and a couple of old baseball caps hung on a set of hooks. On the opposite wall was a cot, covered by a rolled up sleeping bag and a pillow. Right beside it was a small sink and mirror, plus a glass shelf on which was a toothbrush, the remains of a tube of toothpaste, a disposable razor and a shaving brush. It looked as if Carrington had often worked late into the night, then elected to sleep at the office rather than go home. There was even a small dog dish and water bowl on the floor beside the sink. Max turned his attention to the desk, on which sat a very old computer.

It was clear from the material scattered across the desk that Carrington had recently been reassessing all the information he possessed about David

Dexter's disappearance. Max settled into the battered old chair at Carrington's desk and began to quickly sift through the paperwork. An old glossy magazine featured the smiling face of Jonathan Dexter on the front cover, below the headline "Ready for the Challenge". Flipping the page, Max saw an article about Dexter's anticipated run for the presidency. He put the magazine to one side and began studying newspaper clippings on the David Dexter case. Most of them were covered in yellow post-its filled with scribbled notes or numbers. One story mentioned how Vanessa Dexter had been "driven insane with grief" and had been confined to a special hospital. There was even a story about David's funeral after the discovery of his body. It included a brief mention that the police were rumored to have used a psychic to help them locate the grave.

"Who the hell are you?"

Max almost fell out of the chair. A middle-aged man with thinning hair stood in the doorway. He was wearing a heavy tool belt and carrying a large toolbox.

"Not really a place for kids," said the man.

"No," Max replied. "It isn't."

"So what are you doing here?"

"Oh, er," Max stammered, "I'm just getting some stuff for my dad. He asked me to pick it up, but he's so messy. It's hard to find anything on this desk."

The man didn't reply and walked over to the wall near the sink, where he put down his toolbox. Max returned to the papers on the desk. In the margin beside the article about David's grave, opposite the underlined word "psychic", Carrington had written

"Deanna Hastings". He'd also scribbled the words "Tuesday, 10 am coffee". Unfortunately, Max couldn't find any more references to Deanna Hastings or what she and the detective may have discussed.

"Okay," said the man, as he walked back over to the door, "just as long as you know it's going to get pretty noisy once we start drilling into that wall."

Once he'd left, Max found some papers on the desk that he couldn't read. They were written in what looked to be Russian, the odd script being completely unintelligible to Max.

The type of paper indicated that they were cuttings from magazine articles and were accompanied by a photograph of a group of men. Most were wearing white lab coats, but others were dressed in military uniforms. The men were seated around a long boardroom table in what Max assumed was a scientific facility or even a hospital, judging by the equipment visible in the background. The picture reminded Max of photographs featuring Jonathan Dexter on one of the websites he'd viewed at the library.

The caption beneath the photograph in Max's hand identified several of the pictured men, but not all of them. At the top of the frame, Carrington had scribbled "Kovac?" There was also a crudely drawn arrow pointing to one of the participants, a middle-aged man with dark, thinning hair, who was wearing thickly framed glasses.

Max pulled open the desk drawer to find some paper on which to quickly jot down a few notes. There was no notepad in the drawer, only a shallow plastic tray, containing paperclips in a variety of colours, pencils, pens, and a pair of keys on a small metal ring, plus scores of opened envelopes. These mostly contained bills, both paid and unpaid, giving the impression that Carrington wasn't exactly someone who paid attention to detail in his personal affairs.

Sifting through the collection of old mail, Max found an empty envelope, but immediately noticed that it wasn't addressed to Carrington's office, but rather to a PO box number. Max thought that the keys in the drawer were too small for a car or a regular door lock. He guessed that they could possibly belong to a mailbox at a post office. Perhaps Carrington might have kept a few things related to his investigation in a safe, separate place?

Stuffing the envelope and keys into his pocket, Max quickly left the office. As he turned the corner near the building entrance, he almost collided with two police officers.

"Hey," said one of them. "What's your hurry?"

"Sorry," said Max, continuing out into the parking lot.

He had no way of knowing if the officers were on their way to Carrington's office. But by the time they got there, Max would be long gone.

CHAPTER FIVE
PIECES OF THE PAST

JOHN CARRINGTON'S MAILBOX was located at a post office inside a community drugstore only a couple of blocks from his office.

Max made his way along the aisles of the pharmacy to the counter at the back. A young mother with a stroller was being served by a tall slim woman in her late fifties with poorly dyed black hair.

The wall beside the counter was filled with identical narrow, steel mailboxes and it took Max a minute to locate the number matching Carrington's key. He opened the box, reached inside for the contents and pulled them out. There were a few items of personal mail, as well as more bills, plus a letter-sized envelope. Max put everything into the larger envelope and locked the mailbox. The woman at the counter, who now had no customers to deal with, startled him.

"So who are you?" she asked.

"Sorry?" said Max.

"I said, who are you?" the woman repeated. "And what are you doing with Mr. Carrington's mailbox?"

"I'm his grandson," Max replied, thinking quickly. "He asked me to come down and collect the mail."

Glancing nervously at a copy of the morning paper still folded neatly on the counter, Max desperately hoped that the woman hadn't read the story reporting Carrington's death.

"That's funny," said the woman. "He never mentioned a grandson before. Never heard him talk about any family, to tell you the truth. And he's always very chatty when he comes in here."

"Oh well, I, er, don't live around here," Max went on, "and don't see him very often. I'm just here for a few days. He's always really busy with his work as well."

"Sure is," nodded the woman. "He always has some stories to tell too."

"Anyway," said Max, "better be going. Don't want to keep granddad waiting."

The woman just shrugged and said something inaudible under her breath as Max turned to leave. He hurried toward the exit, keeping his fingers crossed that the woman wouldn't pick up the newspaper and see the headline about Max's dear old "granddad" being found dead in the park.

Once he was outside the drugstore, Max spotted a coffee shop on the corner of the next block. He quickly crossed the street, clutching the envelope tightly to his chest. Max ordered one of his favourite cold coffee drinks. He settled in at a table well away from the front windows, where he could examine the contents of the mailbox with some degree of privacy.

From inside the envelope Max pulled out the bills and regular mail, plus a newspaper clipping, a collection of web pages printed from a computer, and some prints of digital photographs. The first paper he examined was a document originating in the local police department years earlier. Although it was a poor quality photocopy, the words "file - not to be removed", were clearly stamped in the top right corner. The document listed a number of missing person cases and how they'd all been thoroughly investigated, with any links between them dismissed. More tellingly, all investigations were to cease forthwith, in compliance with a recent directive from the FBI.

The newspaper clipping from the local paper concerned the recent retirement of a professor at the university. Max read that Aleksander Kovac had worked in research at the university since his arrival from Yugoslavia in the early 1990s. Max had heard of Yugoslavia at school. He'd had a friend in junior high whose family had left there when the civil wars tore the country apart. The picture of Kovac receiving his award from the dean of the university had only been taken a few months earlier. With the connection to Yugoslavia, Max at least partially understood the strange Russian-like script he'd seen at Carrington's office. The old picture Max had seen at the office hadn't been the best quality, but it was definitely an image of the same person as the photograph in the newspaper.

The printed website pages were a selection of

news stories, and Carrington had made extensive notes. The stories, some no more than a headline with a few lines of text, all concerned the deaths of prominent people. There were politicians in the U.S., Russia, and in Europe; nuclear scientists in the Middle East; businessmen and women in the U.S., Canada, Latin America, and Australia; and government officials in over twenty other countries. All of them had died officially of natural causes, although all had apparently enjoyed perfect health. Carrington's scribbled notes seemed to refer to the significance of each of these people, no matter how minor their careers appeared to be, and implied that they were all somehow connected. However, Carrington's notes didn't make much sense to Max.

The printed digital photographs looked to have been taken with a telescopic lens. In the first picture, a tall, slim man was stepping out of a building. His shoulder-length, blonde hair was swept back from his face and he wore sunglasses. In the second photograph, the same man was getting into a white car, accompanied by two other men in dark suits. The pictures weren't very clear and there was no indication of who these people were, just a scribbled letter "K" written in Carrington's handwriting. The dates on the pictures were relatively recent.

Clearly Carrington had been onto something. Yet as far as Max was concerned, the collection of material amounted to only having a handful of the pieces to a jigsaw puzzle, with no completed picture as a guideline to put it back together.

With Carrington now dead, probably no one else suspected anything. Except perhaps Vanessa Dexter, thought Max. Carrington had remarked that David's mother was still alive in a nursing home. She might be completely crazy, but even if she wasn't, Max still had no idea how he'd be able to meet her. And yet he was determined to find out what was going on, even if only for himself.

CHAPTER SIX
BEYOND THE GRAVE

WHEN HE STEPPED out of the coffee shop, Max considered going home and hiding the envelope in his room. Then he thought that it might be useful if he could talk to Mrs. Dexter and back up his story. He checked the Belvedere Gardens website with his phone, noting that they had a barbeque event planned for that day, before making his way to the bus stop.

When he got on the bus, Max sat in one of the seats near the window. In his mind, he went over everything that had happened since he'd been at the cemetery, wondering if he'd ever make sense of it all. Max worried sometimes if there was something seriously wrong with him, although he'd never admit that to his dad. His mother had been depressed and may have taken her own life. He'd overheard his dad talking to his grandmother about it on the phone once. His dad was apparently very concerned that Max would "end up like his poor mother", hence all the visits to medical specialists over the years.

Max held Carrington's envelope close at his side. He still had no idea how he was going to get to see Mrs. Dexter, provided of course she was actually still living at Belvedere Mansions. He also hadn't a clue what the building was like, what kind of access it had, and if there was any type of security system.

Despite all the activity as people got on and off the bus, Max could hardly keep his eyes open. He soon dozed off as he rested his head on the window.

"I don't care who he is. I've never liked him."

"Be reasonable, Vanessa. Aleksander has been working on this project for years and I'm responsible for all the agency's work."

"Reasonable? You're asking me to be reasonable? Does that mean we have to have him here at our house?"

"It's just business and work. It's not like I have a choice, you know."

"There are stories, Jonathan."

"Stories? What sort of stories?"

"About his work, not at the university. They say there's another place where he experiments on people. They say he used to do it back in Yugoslavia and he's doing it here and that you're all covering up for him."

"Vanessa, you're being ridiculous. It's just a regular government research project."

"I just don't think you should be associated with him, Jonathan. Even if it's not true, the rumours alone could wreck your career. Why don't you listen to me? Carrington thinks Kovac's up to his neck in all this."

"Who's Carrington?"

"A detective. He's been tracking Kovac for quite a while. Says he has proof of links between the disappearance of homeless people and children and secret experiments at a place outside of town."

"How do you know all this?"

"I met him and he told me everything. He's been assigned to David's case and thinks there's a connection."

"Vanessa, you really shouldn't talk to people like that."

"Why not? Oh my God, Jonathan, you know there's a connection, don't you? You know what's happened to David, don't you?"

"I never said that."

"Carrington said he suspected you were involved. I can't believe it! You're going to keep it all quiet to safeguard your career! Your own son!"

"Now, Vanessa, listen to reason!"

Max awoke with a start. Someone was sitting next to him and Max found himself staring at a face that was all too familiar.

"Don't say anything, Max, just listen. No one else can see me."

The boy with the thick mop of black hair was wearing the same black t-shirt and pants as when Max had first seen him. He was almost exactly the same height as Max and on his wrist he wore a very expensive watch.

"Rolex," said the boy. "A birthday present from

my parents. You know who I am, don't you, Max? Yes, of course you do."

Max stared into the eyes of David Dexter, paralyzed with fear. The woman in the opposite seat gave Max a curious look, then turned away.

"I don't have much time," said David, "so listen carefully. We've met before, not just when I spoke to you on the bus or when I tried to talk to you outside the coffee shop. When I first made contact, you were too young and I only scared you. I knew I had to wait until you were older. I was your imaginary friend, years ago. You do remember, don't you?"

With a shudder, Max recalled the incident years ago when his imaginary friend had spoken to him. Max had been terrified and had never mentioned the incident to his dad, repressing the jarring memory ever since. Yet he hadn't been able to conceal his subsequent nightmares. Max now knew that his encounter with David Dexter had been the starting point for the visits to a series of doctors, which in turn had led to the lengthy sessions with Dr. Hammond.

"Don't worry, Max, you're not going crazy. I'm real, or as real as I can be for a dead guy. But you know all this, don't you? Hey, don't look so surprised. You've been pretty busy finding out about me, so I figured I should know all about you as well. You might know all about the case, but not all the details. Those are still secret, just like Carrington was going to tell you, if he'd lived long enough. It must be hard to make sense of that stuff in his office and from the box at the post office."

Max clutched the envelope closer to his chest. Glancing at the window, he saw to his horror that

David had no reflection.

"When I was about your age, I accidentally uncovered a top-secret scientific project and, as a witness, I was silenced. As you know, my father was a high-ranking politician with ties to the operation. When I disappeared, I was simply listed as missing and the government scrambled to cover its tracks. Even my own father agreed to stay quiet to save his political career. My mother suspected something wasn't right, but they kept her quiet by saying she was crazy. At first, they put her in an institution for the insane. She's only been in Belvedere Mansions for the last four years, since they figure she's no longer a risk. Hopefully she can answer some of your questions."

The bus lurched as it braked sharply in traffic. As abruptly as he'd appeared, David was gone. Max was still shaken when the bus finally came to a halt. When he stepped onto the sidewalk, Max could hear the music coming from Belvedere Mansions across the road, indicating that the barbeque had started.

CHAPTER SEVEN
VANESSA

As MAX APPROACHED Belvedere Mansions, he could see that all the activity was in the gardens at the rear. The building was a large imposing structure, with a covered area at the front for cars, cabs, and ambulances. The large metal gate leading to the rear of Belvedere Mansions was wide open. There were a couple of employees on duty, checking people as they entered and exited. People also seemed to be showing some kind of tickets or passes to the security people before they were allowed through.

Max could see that the building had a small lobby area. It was staffed by a receptionist, a stocky, middle-aged woman with short, light brown hair and red, thick-framed glasses. There was a door in the wall behind the receptionist's chair, but it wasn't clear whether that led into the interior of the facility. To one side of the reception desk there was a secure door controlled by a keypad. Max knew he might have trouble getting inside. He also knew it would be next to impossible to ask to see Mrs. Dexter if he wasn't related to her.

The receptionist was on the phone when Max entered the lobby. As he approached the front desk, he noticed a small poster on the wall by the security door, advertising the family barbeque event.

"So there's a party today?" he asked the receptionist, as she finished her phone call.

"Yeah," the woman told him, "We're expecting a crowd of relatives, plus all the kids and grandkids are off school now. It's in the gardens at the back, but we've got someone on the gate to stop the old folks wandering off. So do you have a relative living here?"

"What?" said Max.

"A relative," she repeated. "Who are you here to visit?"

"A relative?" said Max. "Oh no, I'm, er, here from my school."

"Isn't school out for summer?" she asked, raising an eyebrow.

"Yeah, but it's like, you know, volunteering," Max lied. "They like us to visit an old folks place and just keep the people company. You know, the ones with no real visitors, sad really. I did a few before school finished, but they arranged some more to keep us kids busy in the summer. Don't want us hanging around on street corners and getting into trouble, do they? They set me up with this place and gave me the woman's name."

"Really," the receptionist said, sounding unconvinced, as she peered at him over the top of her glasses. "First I've heard about it, but still, I'm pretty new here. What was the name?"

"Dexter," replied Max, then tried to sound a little more vague. "Vanessa Dexter, I think."

He pretended to look at where he might have scribbled down the name on Carrington's envelope.

"Okay," she said, "let's take a look. You'll need one of these passes to get by security."

She nodded at a collection of plastic cards with bar codes sitting on the desk. Some had already been placed in envelopes for families who had yet to arrive.

The receptionist negotiated a few pages on the computer screen in front of her.

"Sorry," she apologized, "I'm still getting used to all the names and everything. Oh, there goes the phone again. Hello, Belvedere Mansions. Thank you, I'll put you through."

She turned back to the computer.

"Ah, here we are. What did you say her first name was?"

Before Max could answer, the phone rang again.

"Belvedere Mansions? Yes, I'm sorry, she's on the phone. Would you like to hold? Oh, really? Well, I guess I could just run down there and tell her you're waiting. One moment please."

She turned back to Max.

"Sorry, it sounds like this is pretty urgent. Just a second, I'll be right back."

The receptionist removed her headset, stood up from the desk, and hurried through the doorway behind her chair. Max had no idea how long she'd be gone, so he leaned over the desk, grabbed a pass from one of the envelopes and slipped outside.

As he approached the gate, Max pretended to be talking on his cell phone. One of the staff members had just stepped to one side and lit a cigarette, before ambling over to the sidewalk. At the same time, the other employee was busy chatting to some of the visitors. Max quickly had his pass scanned and then mingled with a group of people as they entered the gardens.

Max figured it would be relatively easy to blend in with the other visitors, some of whom had arrived with children, as they visited aged relatives. It was certainly a busy place. Most of the residents were sitting on lawn chairs or at picnic tables enjoying the sunshine and the band playing under the canopy. Beside the barbeques, there were long tables filled with plates of food, as well as several punch bowls. Max had no idea what Vanessa Dexter looked like, but then he heard a voice.

"Okay, Vanessa, I'll just leave you here. I'll be right back, okay?"

Max spotted an old woman sitting alone at a table in the shade of a broad canopied tree. He cautiously made his way over to the table. There was only one way to find out if this was the right person.

As he drew closer, Max saw that the woman's hair was cut quite short and was dull gray in colour. The woman looked somewhat older than the age Max calculated Vanessa Dexter would be by now. Yet Max saw something familiar in the woman's face. He was convinced that he recognized her from the strange visions he'd experienced about the Christmas presents.

The woman simply stared straight ahead when Max approached and sat down in the chair beside her.

"Hello," he said.

The woman slowly turned to look at him, a vacant expression on her face. Her eyes were almost glassy behind her thin, wire framed glasses, but she said nothing.

"I'm here to visit you."

"Oh, that's nice," remarked an old woman, who was just walking by. "She never gets many visitors, not since her husband died."

"How are you today?" Max asked the woman in the chair.

"You remind me of my son," she said, with a sigh, ignoring his question.

"Really?" said Max.

"Yes, he's about your age," the woman said, then added bitterly, "but he hasn't ever visited me."

"Sorry to hear that," said Max. "Maybe David is just busy."

"I never told you my son's name was David," said the woman.

Her tone was suddenly stern.

"You didn't?"

"No, I didn't," insisted the woman. "Who are you?"

The woman's expression had now completely changed. Her eyes suddenly appeared much brighter. She unexpectedly reached over and grabbed Max tightly by the wrist. He dropped the envelope, the news clipping about Kovac slipping out onto the grass.

"Carrington? And Kovac?"

She gasped, staring in apparent shock at the envelope.

"How do you know Carrington?" she demanded. "Who the hell are you?"

"Please, Mrs. Dexter, relax," said Max. "I just want to ask you a few questions."

"About John Carrington?" she said, raising an eyebrow.

"Only if you want to," replied Max, a little surprised at her answer. "I'll leave anytime you want."

"I saw the piece in the paper about him being found dead in the park," she told him. "One of the women here is obsessed with obituaries. She told me about it."

"Yes, I talked to him just before that."

"How do you know him anyway?"

"I was investigating the David Dexter case," replied Max, "at the library, for a school project. He was on the next computer and we got talking, but there's so much more I'd like to know."

"So you thought you'd come and talk to me, did you?" she said, as she drained her cup.

Max could hardy believe she was being so forthcoming. However, he kept one eye on the rest of the gardens for the staff, just in case Mrs. Dexter changed her mind.

"Ah well, I don't suppose it's going to do any harm now, is it?"

She sounded a little drunk, to be honest, Max thought. There were several empty plastic cups on the table, so he figured she might have been sampling the punch.

"Can you get me another drink?" she asked him. "What did you say your name was?"

"Max."

"Okay, Max," she said. "Can you get me some more punch please?"

"Sure, I'll be right back."

Max went over to the table and ladled out some punch. He kept an eye on Mrs. Dexter, but she didn't seem to be interested in alerting anyone to his presence. Maybe she'd decided to unburden her conscience? She could also be completely out of it, although Max got the impression that Mrs. Dexter was of very sound mind.

"So," Mrs. Dexter said, as Max sat back down at the table, "what is it you'd like to know?"

"I'm just curious about a few things," Max replied. "I know your son disappeared and was later found dead. I'm sorry if that's upsetting for you."

"It still is, to this day," she sighed, "but I'm okay to talk about it now. I usually pretend that I think he's still alive if anyone here asks me about it. If they think I'm crazy, they leave me alone."

"So did you know Carrington well?" asked Max.

"Not really," she replied. "Back then, I was very interested in finding out more about David's disappearance and never gave up hope that they'd find him alive. I heard that Carrington had been working with the police on missing person cases and arranged to meet him. I just figured he might be able to help, even if only to put my mind at ease."

"And did he?"

"Well," Mrs. Dexter said slowly, "he certainly had some interesting theories, that's for sure."

"About Kovac and his projects?" pressed Max. "And your husband was involved in that too, wasn't he?"

"I don't know what you mean," she replied, as she

drained her cup.

"I mean he oversaw a lot of projects," Max explained. "Probably worked with Kovac, at least some of the time?"

"I think you're a little off track, Max," said Mrs. Dexter. "I never said my husband had anything to do with all this. And which school did you say you were doing this project for?"

"How about some more punch?" Max asked her.

"Don't mind if I do," said Mrs. Dexter, with a broad smile.

There was quite a line now for the punch bowl. While he waited, Max occasionally glanced over at Mrs. Dexter's table. People briefly stopped by and chatted with her for a moment of two, although no one ever sat down at her table.

Most of the event's guests appeared to be ordinary families visiting relatives, but Max couldn't help noticing one man in a dark suit. Everyone else at the event was casually dressed.

Max finally got his turn at the bowl and filled the cup. When Max looked over to where Mrs. Dexter was sitting, the man in the dark suit was standing beside her. Mrs. Dexter looked to be very agitated. The man reached into his pocket, pulling out a small object. Max dropped the drink and raced over to the table, barging into several people in the process. Amid angry shouts and protests, he saw the man plunge something into Mrs. Dexter's arm, before quickly walking away.

Max was still only halfway to the picnic table when he saw Mrs. Dexter fall from her chair. By the time Max arrived, the man in the suit was long gone. Mrs. Dexter was surrounded by nursing staff and concerned guests.

"Oh my god, is she okay?"

"I don't know, she's always been a picture of health."

"Stand back please," said a nurse, as she started performing CPR on Mrs. Dexter.

"What happened?"

"One minute she was okay and the next she started to choke," said a young woman, tears streaming down her face.

"Is she going to be okay?"

"No," said the nurse, "I'm afraid not."

"Oh, my god," said Max, under his breath.

"Hey, wait a minute," said a voice behind him.

It was the receptionist.

"Those police officers want to talk to you."

Max turned and ran, avoiding the grasping hands of onlookers as he sprinted to the gate. He burst out onto the sidewalk but didn't get far. A police car was parked directly in his path. Two officers were standing next to the vehicle and one of them raised his hand for Max to stop.

"Are you Max Garrison?" he asked.

"Yes," said Max, with some hesitation, wondering how the officer knew his name.

"Can you come with us to the station please?" the officer said.

He opened the rear door of the police car and invited Max to get in.

"What for?" said Max.

"Some people need to ask you some questions, that's all," said the other officer, as he walked around to the driver's side door.

Max seriously contemplated making a run for it,

but knew that would only mean more trouble. He got into the back of the car and heard an ominous click as the doors locked, sealing him in. The officer who had first spoken to him climbed into the passenger seat and spoke into the radio as the car pulled away.

"Tell Mr. Connor we have Max Garrison and we're bringing him in. We'll be there in about ten minutes."

"Okay," a voice from the radio replied, "I'll let Mr. Connor know."

The men didn't talk with Max on the journey to the police station, during which time Max's mind raced. He knew he'd done nothing wrong. Nevertheless, he was well aware how John Carrington had intimated that people who unintentionally got mixed up in this whole business usually disappeared. Max felt as if he was going to throw up, but struggled to keep it together. Carrington was now dead. Mrs. Dexter had seemed in very good health, but was now dead too. Max couldn't help thinking that he might be next. If they killed David and covered it up, despite his father's role in the government, what chance did Max have?

When they arrived at the police station, the officers ushered Max inside. He was asked to empty his pockets and leave any personal belongings, including his school ID, wallet, and cell phone, with the officer in charge, who also took a note of Max's home phone number.

"Through here please," said the man who'd driven the car.

He gestured for Max to enter a small room, just down the hallway past the front desk.

"Have a seat," he instructed. "Mr. Connor will be right with you."

CHAPTER EIGHT
QUESTIONS

MAX SAT DOWN at the bare table, which had another chair at the opposite side. The room was cold and uninviting and only had one door, beside which was a solitary phone on the wall. Another wall featured a large mirror. Max had seen enough TV and movies to know that someone was likely to be sitting on the other side, watching him right now. They'd doubtless continue to do so throughout his impending interview, looking for any discrepancies in his answers. He could see the mirror out of the corner of his eye, but didn't dare look over at it. Max simply stared straight ahead at the door as he nervously awaited the arrival of Mr. Connor. He felt an odd pressure at the back of his head but put it down to the stress of the situation.

A couple of minutes later, the door opened and

two men dressed in dark suits entered the room. One was tall and willowy with thinning, pale blonde hair, the other was shorter and more heavily built, dark haired with a gray peppered goatee. They looked vaguely familiar, but Max couldn't quite place them.

"Max, I'm Mr. Connor and this is my associate, Mr. Drake," said the blonde man, pulling out a chair on the opposite side of the table and sitting down. "Would you like something to drink?"

Drake remained standing beside the door as Connor handed Max a plastic bottle of water. Max contemplated asking Connor how they knew his name, but thought better of it. Somehow the uniformed police officers had known to watch for him at Belvedere Mansions. They might even be aware of his chat with Carrington. Why else would they have pulled him in?

Max felt the pain in his head again. He took the bottle, but as he opened the water and took a sip, Max realized with alarm where he'd seen these two men before. They'd both been in the photographs that he'd found in Carrington's mailbox. They were also at the coffee shop just after he'd first met Carrington. And although he hadn't seen his face that clearly, Max was convinced that Drake had been responsible for Mrs. Dexter's death.

"So Max," Connor continued, with a warm smile, "we've done a little checking up on you. Just routine, you understand, but can you tell us exactly what were you doing at Belvedere Mansions?"

"It's a school project."

"A school project?" Drake repeated, as he began slowly pacing the room.

"Yeah," Max explained. "We had to choose an old

person to visit."

"Really?" said Drake, sounding unconvinced as he paused only a few feet away from Max's chair. "I've never heard of anything like that."

"Oh, you know," Max told him, "these days, the teachers like to get teenagers involved with the community and doing things with old people. Seems like a good idea, I guess."

Max knew they couldn't easily verify his story with the school, not during summer vacation. Hopefully that would buy him some time.

"I guess we'll have to contact the school board," said Drake, with a smirk. "You'd better hope your story checks out."

"Exactly what do you know about Mrs. Dexter?" Connor asked.

"Who's Mrs. Dexter?" Max replied.

The two men looked at each other briefly, then turned back to focus on Max.

"The old woman you were talking to," Connor continued, as Drake began slowly pacing the room again.

"Oh, okay," said Max. "I never asked her name. I just went there and tried talking to her, just to get my marks for the project. I figured I could get her name later from the nurses to tell my teacher, just to prove I'd been there. She looked lonely and all the other people had visitors. I felt kind of sorry for her."

Max was keenly aware that he was rambling. He hoped that they thought he was just nervous, rather than making it all up as he went along. Yet, each time he answered, Max felt the pressure at the back of his head, like the headache he'd had at the cemetery. There were no images though, so he thought it was the increasingly stressful interview causing the pain.

"So you have no idea who Mrs. Dexter was?" asked Connor.

"No, not a clue," said Max. "Why?"

"Never mind," Drake snapped, this time standing only inches from where Max was sitting. "How do you know John Carrington?"

"Who?" said Max.

"Don't play games with us, kid," said Drake, sternly. "We know you met Carrington the other day at the park."

"Oh, the old guy?" said Max. "I never even asked him his name either. He just seemed to want to chat, that's all."

"What did he want to chat about?" Connor asked.

"Nothing much," Max lied again. "He talked about the park and how it had changed since he was a boy. Then he talked about how much he missed his wife, who'd died recently. It was a bit creepy, to be honest, so I made an excuse and got away as quick as I could."

"You sure that's all you talked about?" Drake demanded.

"Yeah," said Max. "What is he, some kind of criminal?"

"No, nothing like that," Connor assured him.

"So what's this about?" asked Max, innocently. "Am I under arrest or something?"

"No," said Connor, shaking his head, "but we do need to ask you some more questions."

He was about to speak again when the wall phone rang. Drake went over to pick it up.

"This is Drake," he said. "Yeah. That's right. Really? But we just need a few more minutes. I wasn't aware that . . . Okay, if you're sure."

Drake cast a nervous glance first at the mirror, then over at Connor, who appeared equally uneasy. Less than a minute after Drake hung up the phone, the door opened and in walked a tall slim man, with shoulder-length blonde hair. It was the other man that Max had seen in Carrington's photographs. Max also recognized him from the collision he'd had outside the coffee shop.

"I'll take it from here, Drake," the man announced.

"But," Drake began, "we should stay and . . ."

"I said," the man snapped, "I'll take it from here."

He glared at Drake, who looked to be in some visible discomfort. He and Connor hurriedly left the room, closing the door behind them. The man with the blonde hair then sat down at the table in the chair opposite Max.

"So Max," said the man, who Max immediately noticed had very piercing pale blue eyes. "It is Max, isn't it?"

Max simply nodded. He assumed the man was a police officer, although he was very casually dressed in a plain white tee shirt and blue jeans. Max felt very uneasy about this new arrival who was studying him very intensely.

"Don't worry too much about those guys, Max," the man reassured him, with a warm smile. "They're just doing their job and neither of them has kids, so they're not that up on school projects. My name's Kane, by the way."

He extended his hand across the table and Max shook it, offering a weak smile.

"Did you know Mrs. Dexter was a very important

woman?" said Kane.

"No, I didn't," Max answered.

"Her husband used to be an prominent politician," Kane continued. "That's why those guys are looking into why she died so suddenly, checking out who she saw or talked to recently. You know the drill."

Max nodded.

"Then there was that private detective you talked to."

"What private detective?" asked Max.

"Carrington, at the park. Oh, you don't know?"

"He never told me he was a detective," said Max. "I thought he was just some crazy old man, like I told those other guys."

"And now he's dead," said Kane, matter-of-factly.

"What?" exclaimed Max, with mock surprise.

"Dead," Kane repeated. "They found him in the park. The police are still investigating, but it looks like a clear case of death by natural causes. Poor old guy just had a heart attack, they think. But whenever this kind of thing happens, they always look into recent events and you were seen with him in the park. This is just standard procedure."

Up to this point, Kane's tone had been easygoing, friendly even. Then the conversation took a sharp turn.

"So are you fully recovered now, Max?" Kane asked.

"Recovered?"

"From your visits to all those doctors, when you were younger," replied Kane.

"How do you know about that?"

"We make it our business to know these things,"

Kane told him, with a dismissive sweep of his hand.

"Who are *we*?" said Max.

"The police, of course," Kane replied, with a smile that sent shivers down Max's spine. "You've moved schools a lot too, haven't you?"

"What's that got to do with anything?"

"Just trying to get to know a little more about what makes you tick, Max," Kane explained, smiling again.

Max shuffled in discomfort in his chair. How could this guy know so much about him? Could someone get all this from his medical records? And did the police even have the ability or the right to do that at such short notice? After all, he'd only met Carrington recently. They couldn't have been watching him for that long. And were these guys even the police anyway? None of them had introduced themselves with a title like "inspector" or "detective". What was going on?

"Don't worry, you're not in any trouble, Max," said Kane with another pleasant, but deeply unnerving, smile. "This is all standard procedure. Just relax."

Kane's stare became more intense, and he seemed to be concentrating deeply. Max felt his eyelids drooping. Suddenly, it was as if he was on the other side of the mirrored wall. He was watching himself being interviewed by Connor and Drake, then he blacked out. When Max came to, he was still in the chair and Kane was offering him the water bottle. Connor and Drake had returned and were standing over by the door.

"Are you okay, Max?" said Kane. "You passed out there for a moment."

"What happened?" Max asked, feeling decidedly groggy.

"You passed out," Kane repeated. "It's not that uncommon if you're stressed. Do you need the medical officer here at the station to check you over?"

"No, no," Max stammered, shaking his head. "No, I'll be fine. I'm okay."

"Well, if you're sure?" said Kane, handing Max the bottle. "Here, have a drink."

Max took the top off the bottle and rapidly consumed half the contents in a few short gulps. He had a splitting headache, reminiscent of the one he'd experienced when he'd touched the gravestone. He still felt queasy and just wanted to get out of the police station as soon as possible.

"He's clean, Connor," Kane declared, standing up. "You can check up on that story about the school project if you like, but he's pretty mixed up, like we thought when we checked his medical history."

Kane left the room, flashing Max another of his signature smiles on his way out the door.

"Okay, you can go," said Drake.

"You can collect your stuff from the front," Connor added.

Max gathered up his belongings from the officer at the desk, wondering if the uniformed cops were aware of what had happened in the interview room. As soon as he was out of sight of the police station, Max ran, covering six blocks before he felt safe enough to catch his breath. His head was no longer pounding, but his hands were shaking uncontrollably. Two people had likely been murdered, both right after Max had spoken to them.

And now he seemed to be under surveillance himself, either by the police or by someone much more sinister. Max was terrified, but he knew the name of someone who might just be able to help him. It was a long shot, but Max was certain that he was running out of both options and time.

CHAPTER NINE
THE PSYCHIC

FLIPPING THROUGH THE directory in a phone booth, Max discovered that there were several psychic mediums advertising in the local *Yellow Pages*. However, none of them was called Deanna Hastings or even Deanna with a different last name to indicate that she'd got married. Max turned to the *White Pages* and found a fair number of people with the last name Hastings. Only one had the initial D, rather than a full first name, but at least they had an address listed. There was no way to tell if the "D" stood for Deanna or not, but Max knew that it was the only chance he had.

Lacking a pen and paper, Max tore a small section from the phone book containing the address details and headed off on the bus. He changed routes three times, deeming it wise to be cautious after everything that had happened, just in case he was being followed.

The house belonging to the mysterious D Hastings was located in an older part of the city, complete with tall, mature trees and narrow, picturesque streets. The house was virtually hidden behind a six-foot hedge, through which the sole access was a high solid wood gate. A black convertible PT Cruiser was parked on the street outside.

Max gently pushed the gate open, cautiously approached the house and pressed the doorbell. While he waited for someone to answer, Max wondered if he was doing the right thing. He knew very little about Deanna Hastings, except that she'd helped locate David Dexter's body years earlier. Max was very reluctant to explain his dream to anyone or express exactly what he thought was going on. However, he felt that if anyone could help him, it would be someone who claimed to talk to the dead. Max heard footsteps approaching the reverse side of the door, which remained firmly closed.

"Who is it?" said a voice.

"Deanna Hastings?" Max asked.

The door opened just a crack, a sturdy chain preventing it from opening fully. A woman peered out curiously at Max.

"That depends. Who are you?"

"My name is Max. I need your help."

"You have the wrong address," said the woman, beginning to close the door.

"I met David Dexter's ghost," exclaimed Max, throwing caution to the winds. "He told me he was murdered and I have to help him put things right."

The door slowly eased open again.

"What did you say?" the woman asked him.

"David Dexter appeared to me on the bus and spoke to me," said Max. "I've had weird images running through my head too, ever since I touched his gravestone in the cemetery."

"What sort of images?" said the woman, frowning.

"Like pictures from someone else's life," Max replied.

The woman looked very thoughtful for a moment, then slowly lifted the chain and opened the door.

"Come in," she said, softly. "What did you say your name was?"

"Max."

"Okay, Max," said the woman. "I *am* Deanna Hastings. Come through here please."

She led Max along a short hallway, at the end of which a dark wooden staircase wound up to the second level of the house. Max followed Deanna into the sitting room, in which a colourful Turkish rug depicting swirling patterns covered the majority of the hardwood floor. Just inside the doorway stood a tall, antique grandfather clock, which ticked so softly that at first Max wondered if it was even working. Two of the sitting room walls were filled with framed pictures of family members, landscapes, and overseas destinations, where Max assumed Deanna had traveled to on vacation. The other walls contained bookcases crammed with hundreds of books. A wide window overlooked the rear of the house, where the garden was filled with the same type of mature trees that Max had seen on the street outside.

Deanna walked over to the coffee table, which was

flanked by two high-backed easy chairs and a small couch. She gestured for Max to sit on one side of the table, then settled into the chair opposite him. Max waited patiently while Deanna briefly ran her slender fingers though her shoulder-length hair, then her deep brown eyes scrutinized him with an intense stare. Deanna looked to be around forty and Max thought at first that he might have met her before. He then realized that she reminded him of his mother. He also had the uncanny feeling that Deanna Hastings somehow knew that.

"So why have you come to see me, Max?" she asked, with a smile.

"I know you were the one who helped the police locate David Dexter's body," Max replied.

"That was years ago," said Deanna, casually. "Why are you so interested?"

Max took a deep breath and explained everything that had happened after he'd first met John Carrington, including the detective's death, the trip to Carrington's office, the intriguing collection of documents, newspaper clippings, magazine articles and photographs, Vanessa Dexter's death, his interrogation at the police station and, of course, his encounters with David. Deanna listened in silence and appeared completely unfazed by Max's account of his conversations with a ghost. When Max had finished, she stood up and walked over to the window.

"Did anyone see you come here?" she asked, closing the drapes.

"I don't think so," said Max. "Why?"

She rejoined Max at the coffee table and sat down.

"Like it or not," Deanna replied, "you were seen

with two people who just died under mysterious circumstances. It could be you next. And they already hauled you into the police station. Can you describe the man who interviewed you, the one you said you thought had been watching you behind the mirror?"

"He was tall and thin," replied Max, "with blonde hair. He said his name was Kane."

Deanna shuddered.

"Do you know this guy?" Max asked her.

"These people don't fool around," Deanna murmured, gesturing over at the magazine rack beside the couch. "I did see the story about John Carrington in the paper, but hoped it was just some old man dying of natural causes. I thought it was all over."

"What's all over?" said Max, shaking his head.

"You're right," Deanna began, "I did help the police locate the body. Afterwards, I desperately wanted to lay low and in the end I succeeded. I only see people by appointment now and they usually find out about me by word of mouth. Do you know exactly what it is that I do, Max?"

"A little," said Max with a shrug.

"Psychics are a rare breed," Deanna said. "We really don't have any choice about what we are, only in how we decide to use our gift. How old are you, Max?"

"I'm fourteen."

"I was about your age when I discovered for sure what I was," Deanna explained. "I'd sometimes had odd, often impossible, experiences for most of my life up to that point, but I hadn't really thought that deeply about them. I was too busy being a child. Then one day, when I was waiting for a bus on my way home from school, an old woman dressed in old-fashioned clothes sat down on the opposite end of the bench and smiled at me. She seemed strangely familiar, although I was certain we'd never met before. Then she spoke to me and knew my name. She asked me not to be afraid and told me that I had a special gift. She assured me that she and many others were watching over me and would always be there to guide me. When I asked her who she was, she smiled again. I'll never forget that wonderful smile."

"So who was she?" asked Max, intrigued.

"She told me that she was my great-grand-mother," Deanna explained, "and she reached out and touched my hand. Just then, I heard someone shout my name and turned my head to see my friend Nicole approaching the bus stop. When I looked away again, the old woman had vanished. I asked Nicole if she'd seen where the woman had gone, but Nicole simply looked confused. She told me that she hadn't seen anyone and that I'd been sitting alone, looking as if I was talking to myself. Nicole was quite concerned about me, but I told her not to worry and made an excuse about being very tired or something. However, I cried myself to sleep that night. I wasn't scared. In fact, I was remarkably at ease with what I'd learned. It finally made sense of all the strange experiences that had been with me since my early childhood. Although I knew that I wasn't the only one possessing such a wonderful gift, I was always careful to hide it from my parents, who I was certain would never understand. When I was older, however, I discovered that some unscrupulous people had less than noble intentions for someone with my kind of talent."

"What sort of people?" said Max, although he suspected that he already knew the answer.

"Twenty years ago," Deanna continued, "I was a young university student. I was something of a wild child back then. I cut my hair really short and dyed it green, just before my nineteenth birthday. At college, I used to do the occasional psychic reading for my friends. My readings were just for fun, but they came to the attention of people involved in secret experiments on individuals displaying paranormal abilities. One evening on my way home, I was kidnapped. Tests were performed on me, to determine the level of my psychic capability. The scientists wanted to use people like me for military purposes. Doctor Aleksandar Kovac came here from Yugoslavia in the early nineties. Officially, he worked at the university, but was really working on projects for the military."

She paused for a moment.

"Are you okay, Max? You look as white as a sheet."

"In my visions of a laboratory," Max told her, composing himself, "I saw a girl with green hair. That was you, wasn't it? But how could I have such a memory?"

"Because it's not your memory," explained Deanna. "It's David Dexter's. I always thought that he was in that facility and witnessed what was going on, so they killed him."

"So what happened to you?" Max asked.

"After they'd finished," Deanna continued, "they injected me with something and dumped me in Castlegate Park, not far from where I lived back then. Eventually I recalled many of the details, despite their efforts to make me forget everything, but I was too traumatized to go back to university. I never finished my degree. I worked in a number of odd jobs all over the country and never settled. I later returned here and established myself as a psychic medium, but kept a very low profile. At that time, I'd heard of the David Dexter case, of course. With his father being a prominent politician, it was quite famous. One morning, I unexpectedly sensed the location of David's body and informed the police. They were very skeptical at first, but at least they followed up on the information I gave them. As you know, they found David's remains."

"Did you ever meet David's parents?" asked Max.

"I met Jonathan Dexter briefly at the police station," Deanna replied, "and he thanked me for my help. Yet there was much more that I wanted to tell him, so I phoned him that evening. I told him that I'd not only known where David had been buried. I'd also had a strong feeling that he was murdered and that it was somehow linked to the secret government project. Dexter confided to me that they shut the project down after David disappeared. Yet once David's body had come to light, Dexter had his own reasons for being suspicious. He wanted to meet with me, but said that first he had to see a private detective, a man who'd always expressed an interest in his son's case."

"Carrington," said Max.

"I assumed so," Deanna nodded. "However, the next day Dexter was dead, and I was terrified that he'd been silenced. I kept quiet and hoped that no one suspected that I'd ever been in contact with him. Then a few weeks ago, John Carrington contacted me. I was reluctant to talk to him at first, but then I figured it was safe enough after all these years. I arranged to meet him for coffee, but as we both know, he never made it."

"Did he mention what he was working on?" said Max.

"Not specifically," replied Deanna, "but from what you've told me about his office and that mailbox, Carrington was investigating links between those suspicious deaths and the experiments I was subjected to as a young girl, plus all the unsolved missing persons cases. It looks like the project never really stopped. The military might finally have developed a weapon from their work with psychics. I think the project simply went further underground after that and Kovac was still working on it, right up until his recent retirement. Someone called Kane was part of it all back then too. The guy you met at the police station has to be the same man."

"He seemed to know so much about me," said Max.

"Did you experience any strange sensations when Kane was interviewing you?" Deanna asked.

"I had a headache," Max confessed, "and I even blacked out."

"Blacked out?" Deanna repeated. "For how long?"

"I'm not sure, to be honest," replied Max. "Is it important?"

"What did Kane say to the other guys, when he'd finished with you?" Deanna inquired.

"I think he said I was pretty mixed up, or something like that," Max replied. "I don't exactly remember. I just wanted to get out of there as fast as I could."

"Hmm, it sounds like he was probing your mind," said Deanna. "That's why you passed out."

"Probing my mind?" said Max. "What are you talking about?"

"Kane is like me, Max," Deanna explained, "but his psychic abilities have always been much more developed. However, it sounds like he couldn't make sense of these images you've been seeing, the ones that he would have been able to access. Your connection to Carrington and Vanessa Dexter, no matter how innocent it might turn out to be, means they'll be watching you, for a while at least."

"So where do I fit into all this?" Max asked.

"Have you ever seen or even dreamt about David before?" Deanna asked. "Or perhaps about someone you didn't recognize at the time, but who you now realize was him?"

Max shivered even though the room wasn't especially cold.

"My imaginary friend," he replied. "When I was four years old, it seemed as though he'd been around for as long as I could remember. I didn't see him all the time, only when I was alone in my room, either playing or just before I fell asleep. Then on my fifth birthday, I was playing with my new toys in my room after the party guests had left. My imaginary friend was there, but this time it was different."

Max swallowed hard as he struggled to continue.

"Go on," urged Deanna.

"It was as if he was fading in and out," Max continued. "It's hard to describe. He was kind of shimmering. One second he was there and then the next he wasn't. And he was trying to speak to me, which he'd never done before, although I don't remember any words clearly. But I do remember that he reached out and touched me. I'll never forget that icy cold feeling on my hand. I screamed and my dad came to see what was going on, but my imaginary friend had vanished. I never saw him again."

"Until now," added Deanna.

Max nodded.

"I realize now that my imaginary friend was David Dexter, trying to contact me," he confessed. "I've never told anyone about that incident before. It's something I've been desperate to forget ever since it happened. It's always been too painful to remember."

"And that's when your nightmares started?" said Deanna.

"Yes," Max confirmed, "but I never knew the cause. My dad was concerned, so I saw doctors for years and finally ended up at a specialist, but he wasn't really much help. The nightmares started to go away after my seventh birthday. Not long after that, my dad decided I didn't have to see Dr. Hammond anymore."

"But you're always worried he might suggest it again, aren't you," said Deanna.

"I guess so," Max conceded. "That's one of the reasons I'd never tell him about all this. He really would think I'd gone crazy."

"Do you think you're crazy, Max?" Deanna asked him.

"No," said Max emphatically, "I honestly don't. I know I saw David and spoke to him."

"These visions definitely aren't from your life, are they?" Deanna asked.

"No," said Max. "After all that's happened, I'm

convinced that they're part of David's experiences."

"But they don't last long enough for you to make any sense of them, do they? Maybe it's time to dig a little deeper?" Deanna suggested.

"How?" said Max, shaking his head.

"Through something called post-hypnotic regression," Deanna continued. "I can put you under hypnosis and allow you to access memories from another life."

"Is it safe?" said Max, nervously.

"Don't worry," Deanna assured him. "I've done this lots of times. Occasionally there can be something specific that causes distress, but I simply wake the person right away."

"Well, if you're sure," said Max, still feeling a little uneasy.

"Come to the couch," said Deanna, standing up, "and make yourself comfortable."

Max walked over to the couch and lay down.

"Now what?" he said.

"Just relax," Deanna instructed softly. "Now close your eyes and breathe deeply."

Max did as she asked.

"Okay," Deanna went on, "now keep breathing deeply. I'm going to take you back. Just relax, deep breaths."

Max felt as if he were steadily drifting away from the sound of Deanna's voice, which grew increasingly faint, until it was completely gone.

"Are the restraints tight enough?"

"Yes, of course they are. I told you, I know what I'm doing."

"Now keep still, David, this won't hurt a bit."

Max struggled in vain against the sturdy bonds that secured him to the table. Aleksander Kovac's hand moved steadily closer. The hypodermic needle was now only inches from Max's eye. Kane grinned in cruel satisfaction as Max screamed when the point of the needle made contact with his eyeball.

"Max! Max! Are you okay?"

Max was back on the couch.

"Are you okay?" Deanna repeated, looking extremely concerned. "I had to bring you out of it, you were having convulsions. What the hell was going on?"

"I was in David's memories again," gasped Max, sitting up. "Right when he was killed."

"It was a traumatic memory, that's all," Deanna assured him. "Don't worry, it's quite normal."

"But it was so real," said Max. "I could feel the table underneath me and the restraints holding me down. They were as real as this couch, as real as you are!"

He grabbed Deanna's hand tightly.

"It was nothing like a dream or a vision, nothing like them at all!" Max added, starting to panic. "I really felt the needle going in!"

"Are you certain?" Deanna asked, looking alarmed. "That's really unusual."

"You have to send me back again."

"I don't know, Max," Deanna protested. "You really freaked me out just now. I've never experienced anything like that before."

"I need to get further back into David's memories," insisted Max, "before the shock of his death. Can you do that?"

"Of course I can," Deanna confirmed, before adding hesitantly, "but are you sure?"

"It's the only way," replied Max. "David's murder is obviously too much of a barrier. You have to try and deliver me to an earlier point in his life."

"Okay, Max, if you say so," Deanna agreed, "but I'm definitely waking you up at the first sign of trouble. Agreed?"

Max nodded and settled down on the couch, before Deanna repeated her instructions. Once again, Max drifted into semi-consciousness, but he didn't appear further back in David's memories. Instead, Max was walking along a dark tunnel, at the end of which was a brilliant white light. Max could see eerie, shifting shapes in the brightness, but couldn't quite bring them into focus. Then he heard someone speak to him.

"It isn't your time. You must go back."

Max didn't recognize the soothing voice. Yet at the same time he sensed an odd connection to the speaker that he couldn't explain.

"What is this place?" said Max. "Where am I?"

The voice simply repeated the words.

"It isn't your time. You must go back, but to the beginning. You must put things right."

Then suddenly the light vanished and Max was back, but not to where he'd expected to be.

CHAPTER TEN
BEING DAVID

MAX WAS STANDING in a beautiful sitting room, containing luxurious sofas and elegant furniture, some of which looked antique. A polished black grand piano stood in front of a large window, outside of which lay a wide gravel driveway framed by rows of tall cedars. On the wall to his right a shelf was filled with framed photographs. One showed David Dexter and his classmates wearing their school uniforms with the school building behind them. A polished trophy stood next to the picture. Max crept over to the shelf. It was a rather nondescript metal cup, but on the plinth underneath was written "First Place - Piano Competition", along with something in Latin that Max couldn't understand.

This was unbelievable. Had Deanna really sent him back into the past? Max heard a noise from upstairs. David's parents! On the shelf, there were several pictures of Mr. and Mrs. Dexter and at one end of the shelf were two photographs of David. In the first one, he was on a boat standing beside a suntanned middle-aged man who was holding an enormous fish. The palm trees in the background indicated a tropical location. Max recognized the boat and the accompanying scenery from his visions. In the second photograph, David was at a ski resort standing next to a girl with shoulder-length blonde hair. Then in the glass of the frame, Max saw his own reflection.

He started to hyperventilate and felt like he was going to throw up. Across from the bottom of the staircase, the door to the bathroom was slightly ajar. He darted over, closed the bathroom door and locked it. He leaned against the door, his mind still reeling, although his breathing was returning to normal.

An ornately framed mirror hung on the wall over the sink and Max was astonished at what he saw. Staring back at him was the face of David Dexter, the thick mop of black hair almost completely obscuring his blue eyes. Max ran his fingers up and down his face, cautiously pinching his cheeks to determine if he was dreaming. On Max's wrist was the Rolex watch David had talked about on the bus and he was dressed in a black tuxedo. It was incredible. Deanna's hypnosis had actually worked. Max had traveled back in time and into another life. Max felt like his head was going to explode, but he knew he certainly couldn't hide in the bathroom all evening. He swallowed hard and opened the bathroom door.

"David? Are you ready to go?"

Max spun around to see Vanessa Dexter coming

down the winding staircase, looking considerably younger than when he'd last seen her at Belvedere Mansions. She had sparkling blue eyes and her hair was a deep chestnut brown, cascading over her shoulders.

"Well?" she said.

"Oh, yeah," said Max, haltingly. "I'm ready."

"Good, the car should be here any minute. I hope this is all worth it."

Max turned and immediately recognized Jonathan Dexter as he walked into the room, having seen him in so many photographs during his research. Mr. Dexter was a tall, slim man, possessing an air of authority, his jet-black hair graying slightly at the temples.

"Now, Jonathan," said Mrs. Dexter, as she gave him a quick peck on the cheek, "you know how important these functions are. It was very good of Carl to go to all this trouble, you know."

"Ha!" laughed Mr. Dexter. "Carl Maurier can afford to have a party like this every week. And he wouldn't be hosting it if there wasn't something in it for him, you know that."

Max felt a strange sensation behind his eyes and must have appeared in some discomfort.

"David, are you feeling all right?" Mrs. Dexter asked, looking rather concerned.

"Perfect," said Max, with a nod, although he wondered what he had got himself into.

"The car's here," Mr. Dexter announced.

Max looked out the window and saw a black limousine outside the front door.

"Okay," said Mr. Dexter, "let's get moving."

Max followed David's parents as they left the

house.

"Good evening, Mr. Dexter, Mrs. Dexter," said the driver, opening the rear door as they approached the car.

"Good evening, Sean," Jonathan replied, as he stood aside to allow his wife to get into the back seat.

"Hi, David," said Sean, with a smile.

Max was startled when images from what he had to assume were David's past life experiences flashed across his mind. It appeared that Sean had worked as a driver for the Dexter family for several years and had often driven David to school when he was younger. Max got into the car, struggling to keep David's memories in check.

As the car swept along, Max marveled at the large and luxurious houses of the Dexters' upscale neighbourhood, a world away from the surroundings of his own home. The limousine left the residential area, driving by a restaurant whose neon sign had just been extinguished as it closed for the evening. Max was sitting between Mr. and Mrs. Dexter, who talked constantly to each other throughout the journey, but Max wasn't really listening. He found that he was remembering countless episodes from David's life—his childhood, family holidays, his friends at school, the occasion that he'd fallen off his bike and broke his ankle at the age of seven. As more of David's memories flashed across his mind, Max desperately hoped that his own personality wouldn't be completely swamped in the process.

When his thoughts finally cleared a little, the car was heading into the downtown area. Max noted that the city skyline looked different from what he was familiar with, since numerous office and apartment towers would be built in the coming years. When the car came to a stop outside a large hotel, Sean opened the rear door. Mr. Dexter got out first, followed by Max, then Mrs. Dexter

"Hurry up, David," urged Mrs. Dexter. "We don't want to keep everyone waiting."

Max followed David's parents through the revolving door as they crossed the marble floor of the hotel lobby, passing under glittering crystal chandeliers. He'd seen the exterior of this hotel a few times times before, but had never actually been inside. Max couldn't help being impressed by the sheer luxury of it all as he accompanied Mr. and Mrs. Dexter towards the staircase. Inside the ballroom, Max again marveled at his opulent surroundings, gazing up at the elevated ceiling from which hung more ornate chandeliers. The dinner party was in full swing, filled with men dressed in tuxedos and women wearing elegant evening gowns. Max stepped to one side as a waiter hurried by him carrying a tray filled with sparkling champagne glasses.

"Come on, David," said Mrs. Dexter, grabbing his wrist. "There are some people we need to say hello to."

For the next half an hour, Max was introduced to at least thirty men and women in and around the main ballroom, all friends of Mrs. Dexter. It was obvious to Max that she was extremely proud of her son. Although in his own time Max knew that she'd been falsely committed to the hospital, supposedly driven mad with grief, he could see that her son's death must have hit Mrs. Dexter incredibly hard.

At the far end of the ballroom, Max spotted Mr. Dexter talking to a middle-aged man with thinning brown hair, plus two other men in military uniforms. To Max's relief, Mr. Dexter beckoned him over. After Max had made his apologies to Mrs. Dexter and the others, he went over to where Mr. Dexter was standing.

"General Travis, Colonel Marshall," Mr. Dexter said, when Max arrived, "you remember my son?"

"Of course," said the General, extending his hand. "How are you, David?"

"Good, thank you," said Max

He shook Travis' hand, while the Colonel simply smiled in greeting.

"And David, do you remember Dr. Kovac?" Mr. Dexter asked. "He's been to our house for dinner a few times, when you were younger, but perhaps you've forgotten."

"Yes, it's been a while," said Kovac, offering his hand.

Max immediately recognized Aleksandar Kovac from the photographs he'd retrieved from Carrington's office and mailbox. Yet, the instant Max's fingers brushed against Kovac's palm, Max realized that he actually knew the doctor very well indeed. Suddenly, images of a scientific facility, complete with men and women in white lab coats, flooded into his mind. Max heard the screams of victims and saw Kovac standing over a young woman with green hair who was lying on a table. Abruptly, Max pulled his hand away.

"David?" said Mr. Dexter. "Is everything all right?"

"Yes, yes," stammered Max. "I was, er, just

thinking of the last time I saw you, Dr. Kovac. Yes, that's it. You're right. It has been a while. If you'll excuse me, I'm just going to get some fresh air."

Finding it difficult to breathe, Max quickly left the ballroom. He hurried back down the staircase and across the lobby to the front entrance. He stood on the hotel's front steps, greedily gulping in the night air. The memories Max had experienced when he touched Kovac's hand had been frighteningly vivid. As he watched the downtown traffic, his breathing gradually returned to normal.

"What are you doing out here?" said a voice behind him.

Startled, Max turned around. It was Mrs. Dexter.

"Oh," Max answered, "I, er, just needed some fresh air."

"Well, don't stay out here too long," said Mrs. Dexter, turning to go back inside. "You look a little pale."

"Okay," said Max, with a smile. "I'll see you later."

As he watched David's mother stroll back across the lobby, a cool breeze made Max shudder. He decided to take Mrs. Dexter's advice and return to the party. However, Max really didn't want to meet any more of her friends. He avoided the ballroom and made his way along a corridor that was mercifully quiet. When he passed a room to which the door was slightly ajar, he heard Mr. Dexter's voice. Through the crack in the door, Max could see David's father, the two military officers, and Aleksandar Kovac engaged in a heated discussion.

"What do you mean cancel the project?" Kovac fumed.

"I'm sorry, Aleksandar," said Mr. Dexter, "but we

told you what would happen if these abductions continued. We could only cover it up for so long and now the police are taking an interest again. For God's sake, we're still dealing with the fallout from people who went missing years ago, especially the children."

"You never cared much before," Kovac sneered, turning to Colonel Marshall. "Didn't you say that the end justified the means, Colonel? What's the matter? Are your bosses in Washington giving you some heat?"

"The project has simply run its course," said Colonel Marshall, with a disarming smile. "You know how these things are."

"Doctor Kovac," added General Travis, "your research and subsequent work has all been invaluable, but we have all we need."

"You can't do this!" Kovac protested. "I'm so close to a major breakthrough! What about that girl we grabbed at the university last week?"

"Aleksandar," said Mr. Dexter, "I'm sorry. These disappearances have drawn far too much attention. We can't afford for this to be exposed. Once you've finished with the subjects you have at the moment, we have to close everything down at the end of the month. All traces at the old navy warehouse will be erased. There's nothing you can do."

"Isn't there, Mr. Dexter?" said Kovac, slowly. "We'll see about that."

Max stepped back as Kovac headed for the door and flung it open, storming out of the room. He immediately noticed Max in the hallway and fixed him with an icy stare.

"Ah, David, isn't it?" he said, barely concealing a snarl. "I hope you're enjoying yourself tonight, although it seems the party's over."

Max watched Kovac hurry down the staircase. He had the peculiar sensation that he'd witnessed this very scene before and guessed that this was perhaps what David must have experienced. The intermittent flashes of memories, combined with the struggle to keep his own thoughts in check, were giving Max a headache. He decided to find Mrs. Dexter and ask if they could leave the party early.

Max made his way through the crowd in the ballroom. He finally spotted David's mother and politely interrupted her as she stood chatting with a couple Max had met earlier that evening.

"Is it okay if we go now?" Max asked her. "I'm really not feeling very well."

"Really?" said Mrs. Dexter, making her excuses to her friends. "You poor thing. Not a problem, I'll just let your dad know. Why don't you go and wait outside and get some air? I'll see you in a few minutes."

As he stood outside the hotel entrance, Max thought to himself how David's perfect life would soon all come crashing down. Or would it? Max couldn't help but second-guess himself, wondering exactly how his own presence here in the past within David's body and mind would affect the course of events. Surely with his knowledge of what was to come, Max could change things for the better? David could be saved, couldn't he? Perhaps that was why Max had been allowed to come back in time?

"There you are," Mrs. Dexter said, as she waved in the direction of the limousine parked a little farther down the street.

The car slowly drove to where Max and Mrs. Dexter were standing. Sean got out to open the rear door.

"Is Mr. Dexter not joining us?" he asked.

"No, Sean," replied Mrs. Dexter, "he's coming along later. David's not feeling too well, so we thought we'd get an early night."

"Sorry to hear that, David," Sean smiled, as Mrs. Dexter climbed into the back seat. "I hope you'll feel better in the morning."

"Thanks," said Max.

Once Max was in the car, Sean closed the door. The limousine pulled away from the sidewalk and slowly eased into the traffic.

"So is it a headache?" Mrs. Dexter asked.

"What?" said Max.

"Is it a headache?" she repeated. "You said you weren't feeling well. I just wondered what it was."

"Oh, yeah," Max replied, with a weak smile. "A bit of a headache."

He faked a frown, attempting to appear in as much pain as possible.

Mrs. Dexter seemed to get the message, smiling back at him and briefly squeezing his hand. The rest of the journey was undertaken in silence. As soon as they got home, Max told Mrs. Dexter that he simply wanted to get an early night. She looked a little concerned, but nevertheless satisfied that there was nothing seriously wrong.

Max went straight upstairs, instinctively knowing where David's bedroom was located. When he flicked on the light, Max immediately noticed how tidy the room was in comparison to his own. Yet he saw so many things from David's life that felt familiar—the posters of contemporary bands and sports personalities adorning the walls and the baseball glove on top of the bureau. Five shelves filled with books that Max instantly had recollections of reading. On another shelf by the window was a model ship. Max knew that David had built it when he was nine years old, while also acknowledging that he would never have had the patience to construct it himself. The desk was conspicuously lacking the disorganized pile of papers and folders Max was used to seeing in his room. On the edge of the desk, a reading lamp stood beside a framed picture of David with his grandparents.

There was no small TV and no video game cases lying around either. Max noticed the absence of a computer. He knew that home computers simply weren't that common yet in this time period. Similarly, there was no evidence of a cell phone, an essential item for just about everyone in Max's own time. Although there was no cellphone or similar digital music device, Max picked up the CD player from David's desk. This was something Max was familiar with, since his dad still had one, never used these days, in the glove compartment of his truck. There was also a set of keys on the desk, along with a wallet, containing around sixty dollars in cash, plus a collection of plastic, including membership cards, and two bankcards.

Max's headache intensified as he once again fought to keep in check the images filling his mind. He lay on the bed, growing increasingly concerned if he would continue to remember his real life. Or perhaps eventually he'd be unable to distinguish one existence from the other? Maybe, Max pondered, it was only a matter of time before he lost all recollection of the future and actually became David Dexter? As he thought of the picture beside the reading lamp, Max was keenly aware that grandparents had never been a part of his own life. The contrast between David's family and his own were also painfully obvious to him. David had two loving parents who were successful, rich and had a very comfortable lifestyle. It was certainly very tempting for Max to simply forget his less than perfect life in the future and somehow become David Dexter.

Yet was he inevitably doomed to repeat the tragic events of the past? Max had already met Kovac. He'd heard him mention a girl from the university that Max was convinced was the young Deanna Hastings. Max wanted to locate the secret scientific facility and learn more, yet suspected that David might have done exactly the same thing and then lost his life. Could Max even change what had happened before? Was everything fated to occur, no matter what he did?

Max was extremely reluctant to succumb to sleep, wondering if by morning he'd be marooned in the past. Yet as hard as he struggled to keep his eyes open, it wasn't long before he fell asleep.

CHAPTER ELEVEN
THE DETECTIVE

THE NEXT MORNING, Max was disoriented when he woke up, but relieved that he remembered who he really was. He sat up, still wearing the formal clothes from the night before. It looked as if someone, probably David's mother, had come in to check on him the previous evening and closed the curtains. Max got up and searched through David's closet for something more appropriate to wear, selecting a pair of jeans and a plain black tee shirt. It seemed appropriate since that was what David had been wearing when Max had met him in the future. Once he was dressed, Max went downstairs. The house was quiet and there was a note from Mrs. Dexter attached to the fridge.

"Hi David. Hope you're feeling better. We thought we'd just let you sleep in this morning.

Dad's gone out to an appointment, something to do with work. I'm only over at Aunt Carol's, so call me if you need anything. I should be back just after lunch. See you later. Mom."

When Max finished reading the message, the mention of Mr. Dexter's appointment triggered something in his mind. He had a vague recollection of being in the car with David's father, although he couldn't recall where they'd been going. He also recalled saying goodbye to Mr. Dexter, after he was dropped off somewhere. Max strongly suspected that David must have traveled to the secret facility that very morning.

Max now knew for certain that he could change David's fate. Since David hadn't accompanied his father, the same events obviously weren't predestined to occur. Max briefly considered the risks that might be involved in changing the past, but brushed them aside. His very presence here, courtesy of Deanna's hypnosis, had already changed things.

Max glanced over at the clock on the kitchen wall. It was only just after nine and he had several hours before Mrs. Dexter returned. Max had no idea how he would even find a scientific facility, but he knew someone who just might be able to help him.

He remembered that Carrington had been working with the city police at the time of David's disappearance. Max's first instinct was to search online, but remembered that the Dexters didn't have a home computer. Max searched though several of the kitchen drawers until he found the local phone directory, next to a small glass jar filled with loose change. Once he'd located the number, he called the city's main downtown police station. While they had no John Carrington on their staff, the woman at the reception desk was very helpful and told Max that the detective worked out of another office. She wasn't able to transfer Max, but gave him the number to call. Max thanked her as he put down the phone then called the other office. His hands were trembling as he punched the digits on the keypad. After just two rings, another woman answered and Max asked to be put through to Detective Carrington. Max took steady, deep breaths while he waited for the call to connect.

"John Carrington," said the detective in a very businesslike tone.

"Hi, Mr. Carrington," said Max, struggling to prevent his voice from quivering. "My name's David and I have some information that you may be interested in."

"Who is this?" Carrington asked him. "What did you say your name was?"

"My name's David Dexter," Max continued, trying to remain calm. "You may have heard of my father?"

"Jonathan Dexter?" asked Carrington, sounding decidedly unconvinced. "Is this some kind of joke?"

"It's no joke, Mr. Carrington," Max replied. "I've some information that I think you'll find very interesting. It's about the missing person cases you've been following."

"What about them?" Carrington demanded.

"About their connection to the university," said Max.

"Okay," said Carrington, slowly, "so tell me about it."

"Not on the phone," Max replied. "Can we meet?"

"Sure, why not," Carrington agreed, after a slight pause, to Max's surprise. "Where?"

"There's a restaurant near where I live."

"Yeah, I think I know the one," Carrington said. "Mickey's, right?"

"Yes, that's it," said Max, relieved that he'd remembered enough of the neon sign from the previous evening.

"So what time can you be there?"

"Say in half an hour?" said Max.

"This better be serious," said Carrington, sternly.

"Oh, it is," Max assured him, "don't worry about that."

"Okay then, see you there," said Carrington, hanging up.

When Max put down the phone, his hand was trembling. Although he occupied David Dexter's body, Max had to admit that he had no idea if he could pull off the elaborate deception. However, he steeled himself for the task ahead, knowing that John Carrington was perhaps the only person who could help him.

Max put the phone book back in the drawer. He grabbed a handful of coins from the jar, before he remembered that David's wallet was on the desk in the bedroom. He went upstairs, grabbed the wallet and the keys then left the house to meet with John Carrington.

From his connection to David's memories, Max somehow seemed to know the direction to Mickey's restaurant as soon as he stepped out of the front door of the Dexters' house. The Dexters lived in a neighbourhood that Max had never visited in his own time. Most of the houses were huge, with extensive lots, professionally landscaped gardens, and double or even triple garages. The streets were lined with tall, mature trees and carefully trimmed lawns, hedges, and shrubs. It was a far cry from the collection of drab apartments and condos that dominated the area where Max and his father lived in the future.

As he walked, Max pondered how much information he could actually disclose to Carrington. He knew that he'd have to be careful what he told the detective, in case Carrington grew suspicious as to how David Dexter knew so much. As a detective, Carrington was no doubt highly experienced in questioning suspects and probing for weaknesses in an alibi. Max resolved to be selective in what he revealed, while attempting to assess exactly how much Carrington already knew about Kovac's operation.

When Max entered the restaurant, the first thing he noticed was the smell of cigarette smoke drifting through the air. He glanced around as he approached the counter and saw that some of the customers were smoking cigarettes as they chatted over coffee. It was something that Max never experienced in his own era, where smoking was unwelcome just about everywhere. At the cash register, Max bought a small soda and was pleasantly surprised at how cheap it was. The handful of change he'd taken from the kitchen jar was more than enough. As he walked away from the counter, Max wondered if he'd be able to recall David's PINs for the bankcards, but figured he had some cash, if needed.

He settled into a booth by the window. As he

watched the traffic, Max began to appreciate how greatly things would change in the coming years. The cars he'd seen in the Dexters' neighbourhood had all been relatively new for their time. Yet as Max watched the period vehicles in the parking lot, many seemed positively ancient to him.

He studied people as well, marveling at how some fashions or hairstyles sometimes resembled those of his own time period, while others looked bizarrely different. Max also noted the absence of music seeping down from overhead speakers, something that seemed all pervasive in his own time. It was similarly strange not to hear the endless variety of ring tones from cell phones that permeated so much of life in the future.

"David?"

Max looked up to see a man in his mid-forties standing beside the table, holding a steaming cup of coffee.

"Yes."

"John Carrington," said the man

He gave Max a brief smile before settling into the seat opposite and lighting a cigarette.

Max easily recognized the younger version of the man he'd last talked to in Castlegate Park. Carrington had thick brown hair, but a goatee didn't yet frame his mouth. His face was thinner, almost drawn. He wasn't wearing glasses, although the dark circles under Carrington's eyes indicated he'd probably spent too many late nights working at the office.

"Okay, David," said Carrington. "I've got to admit I was a little skeptical when you called, but I can at least see that you're really who you say you are. I've seen your picture in the paper before, with your parents. Now, I'm a busy guy and I don't have much time. First of all, why did you call me? What do you know about these missing person cases?"

"I heard you were investigating them," Max replied. "I thought you'd be interested in what I know."

"And what do you know, exactly?" Carrington asked him, studying Max's face intently.

Max took a sip from his drink then began telling Carrington about what he'd heard at the dinner party. He even included snippets of information that he'd learned in the future, such as details about Kovac's experiments with psychics, in order to make the story all the more plausible. Carrington regarded him quizzically throughout. Max wasn't entirely sure whether the detective believed him or merely felt that he was playing some kind of practical joke.

"And you say that it was Dr. Kovac and two military guys who were there with your father?" he said when Max had finished.

"Yes, and they mentioned some old navy warehouse."

"I knew it," said Carrington smacking the surface of the table with the palm of his hand. "That would explain so much."

"So what are you going to do?"

"I think I know which place they've been using," replied Carrington. "I'll go and check it out for myself."

"Can I help?" said Max.

"This isn't a game, David," Carrington told him. "It's not something for kids to get involved in."

"I'm fourteen," said Max.

"Look, David," Carrington said, calmly, "I'm very grateful for the information. This is all very fascinating, but I have to admit I'm still skeptical. And I'm still not sure why you'd want to tell me all this, since your dad is part of the whole thing, as far as I can tell. If this becomes public knowledge, his political career will be ruined. He can kiss goodbye to a run for the White House."

"I think he's considering leaving politics anyway," said Max.

"Really?" Carrington asked. "I didn't see anything in the news."

"It's, er, private really," Max lied, knowing that he couldn't possibly explain Jonathan Dexter's future career path without revealing his own true identity. "I know he and my mom have talked about it. They think the stress of a campaign will be too much and they want their privacy."

"Well, I can understand that," Carrington nodded.

"So could Jonathan's," Max began to say before correcting himself, "I mean, my dad's name be kept out of all this, if it becomes public?"

"That might be tough," confessed Carrington, "but then again, even if what you're saying is true, it's unlikely it will *ever* be made public. Ever since I started trying to make a connection to the missing person cases and some kind of secret operation, I've come up against roadblocks at the police department. Even if I expose this, the government may just throw Kovac to the wolves and let him take the blame. Your dad probably won't be implicated at all. And if he's leaving public life anyway, there isn't too much to worry about."

"So he won't be involved?"

"I can't promise anything, but I'll do what I can," said Carrington, extinguishing his cigarette in the table's ashtray as he stood up. "Now, you'd better run along home. Thanks for the information."

"But I can help," Max insisted as he followed Carrington outside to where the detective's red pickup truck was parked.

"Like I told you," said Carrington, as he opened the driver's door, "thanks for the information but there isn't anything else you can do."

He patted his jacket pockets.

"Damn. I left my lighter and smokes in there. Just go home, David."

Carrington turned away and went back into the restaurant, leaving Max standing on the sidewalk. Maybe he should just leave it up to Carrington and the police? After all, Carrington may now have more information that he would have done if Max hadn't traveled back and talked to him. As far as Max knew, David and Carrington had never met at Mickey's in the previous timeline, since once again, events had been changed. Perhaps he should just go home, although Max felt he almost had a duty to help expose Kovac and bring him to justice. Max noticed the blue plastic tarp in the back of the truck. Maybe he could help out after all, even if Carrington wasn't exactly inviting him to tag along? Max went to the rear of the truck, climbed in and pulled the tarp over himself just before Carrington emerged from the restaurant.

CHAPTER TWELVE
ON THE WATERFRONT

IT WASN'T TOO far to the waterfront, but the back of the truck was extremely uncomfortable. It appeared Carrington was something of a handyman outside his detective work. The truck bed was filled with tools, some loose and some packed away neatly. There were also pieces of wood, ceramic floor tiles, a medium sized bag of what looked like cement, and cans of paint and varnish, none of them particularly safely stacked.

Each time they stopped at a set of traffic lights Max could hear the radio playing through the small sliding window that was open at the back of the cab. The songs that had been hits in the mid-'90s, along with songs from earlier eras, were a little familiar to Max from some of his video games and movies. Max kept thinking about what he'd got himself into but knew he had no choice but to see it through.

Eventually, the truck slowed down and took a sharp turn to the left. The road became extremely bumpy and Max struggled to stop some of the heavier items in the truck bed from falling on him. Eventually the truck came to a stop and the engine was turned off. Cautiously, Max peered out from under the plastic tarp as much as he dared.

Twenty years in the future, the waterfront had been completely renovated, becoming a trendy shopping district. Back in the time of David Dexter, it was still a dismal, rundown industrial area, filled with rusting cranes and abandoned warehouses. This particular part of the waterfront was completely deserted. Most of the buildings looked as if they hadn't been in use for several decades.

To the right, there was a long steel building with an arched roof, beside some single story wooden structures that appeared to be interconnected. A high chain-link fence topped with barbed wire surrounded the buildings. There was a sliding security gate built into the fence, but it was firmly closed. A white van, with *Richardson's Heating and Refrigeration* written on the side in red lettering, was parked next to the main building.

Carrington was taking a drink from a plastic bottle and looked to be talking on a radio. His attention wasn't on the rearview mirror, so Max clambered out of the truck bed. He wasn't exactly sure what he was going to do, except get somewhere safe and plan his next move. He crept along the side of the truck, intending to dart across to the nearest building, but Carrington spotted him.

"What the hell?" he demanded, as he burst out of the cab. "Where did you come from? Were you in the back of the truck?"

"I told you I could help," replied Max.

"And I told you this isn't a game, David," Carrington snapped. "This could be really dangerous. This is no place for kids."

"I'm fourteen," Max shot back indignantly.

"Look," Carrington continued, "you can't be here, David, and what the hell would your father think? This is nuts, just nuts."

Carrington shook his head in disbelief, turning away. As he did so, Max saw the security gate slide open. Two men emerged from the main building and hurried towards Carrington's truck. One of the men carried a rifle.

"Great," said Carrington, "what do these guys want? Okay, just stay calm and let me do all the talking."

They both remained still a few feet from the truck as the men approached. As they drew closer, Max instantly recognized younger versions of Connor and Drake, who was holding the rifle, but not pointing it directly at them. Connor had a pistol in a holster attached to his belt.

"Who are you?" Connor demanded. "What are you doing here?"

"Just got lost," shrugged Carrington.

"Yeah, we took a wrong turn," Max added.

"Who are you, kid?" asked Drake.

"I'm his nephew," lied Max.

"Got any ID?" Connor asked Carrington.

"Sure," said Carrington.

While Drake nervously toyed with the rifle,

Carrington slowly reached into his pocket and pulled out his wallet, handing it to Connor.

"Check this out," said Connor, showing Drake the private detective's ID.

"Okay," said Drake, "you're both coming with us."

The journey to the arched metal building was undertaken in silence. Connor and Drake, the latter keeping a firm grip on the rifle, remained focused on Carrington, with only the occasional glance at Max. He realized there was a fair chance that he and Carrington might not get out of this alive. Hoping that the men's attention would remain focused on Carrington as they approached the metal building, Max readied himself to run. His plans were interrupted, however, as they arrived at the entrance, where a tall slender woman wearing a white lab coat was standing.

"So who are these guys?" said the woman.

"He says they were just lost," Connor told her, "but this guy's a private dick."

He handed the woman Carrington's wallet, open to his ID.

"And who's the boy?" she asked.

"His nephew."

"Does he have any ID?" said the woman, frowning as she studied Max's face.

"I never checked him," Connor admitted, then told Max, "Give me your wallet."

Max reluctantly reached into his pocket, pulled out his wallet. He handed it to Connor, who immediately passed it to the woman.

"Well, well, David Dexter," the woman said icily, before giving Max back the wallet. "I thought you looked familiar. Take them inside. I'm sure Doctor Kovac will be pleased to see them."

As she turned back into the building, Drake lowered the rifle slightly. Carrington pushed Connor over then swung a fist at Drake, who dropped his weapon.

"Run, David!"

Max ran, but Carrington was knocked to the ground. Max glanced over his shoulder and saw Connor hit the detective on the head with the butt of the rifle, before Drake kicked Carrington in the stomach.

Max kept running until he reached the nearest wooden building. There wasn't much inside, just a few old oil drums along the walls. There was some rusting industrial equipment in the far corner, where a small door led back outside. The building also had an upper level, accessed by a ladder.

Max went over to the small door and eased it open slightly. He watched Connor and Drake take Carrington inside the steel building. Max was certain that it wouldn't be long before they came looking for him too. He had no idea what he was going to do. He could try and get help, but had no idea how far he was from the main road. Max knew that he had no choice but to attempt to rescue Carrington.

CHAPTER THIRTEEN
PROJECT MINDSTORM

PEERING OUT OF the side door, Max confirmed that the steel building was relatively close. Yet before he could make a run for it, Connor and Drake emerged with two other men and headed in his direction. If Max ran across the open area, they'd spot him for sure. He'd have to wait until they were almost at the building's main entrance then slip out the door. Max held his breath as the men came closer. When they were just about to enter the building, Max gently pushed open the side door and raced for the steel building.

Five cars were parked inside. Otherwise the building was almost completely empty, apart from some old wooden crates stacked along the far wall. There was no indication where Carrington might have been taken. Before Max could explore further, he heard a vehicle approaching. Max darted behind the crates as a car entered the building and parked. A man around the same age as Kovac, with thick gray hair and dark rimmed glasses, stepped out of the car and walked through a doorway. Max hurried over to see where the man had gone and discovered that the door led into the interconnected buildings.

The corridor ahead of him was empty. Max crept along the hallway, hoping to find where Carrington was held captive. The first room Max found had a single chair in the centre and a row of filing cabinets beside a desk near the door. The bottom drawers of the cabinets were open and empty. When Max looked inside the other drawers, there was nothing in them either. There were, however, a few file folders on the desk. Max gasped as he opened the first one.

It contained information similar to what he'd found in Carrington's mailbox, about mysterious deaths around the world. This was clearly when the operation had still been in the planning stages. It was all connected to something called *Project Mindstorm*. There were memos and other documents marked confidential from government departments, mentioning Jonathan Dexter, Kovac, and military officers. Before Max could read any more, he heard footsteps approaching. He quickly hid behind the filing cabinets, crouching down as he heard a familiar voice.

"Is Kane on his way?"

Peering out from his hiding place, Max saw Kovac and the man who'd arrived in the car. Both were wearing white lab coats.

"Yes, he shouldn't be long," replied Kovac's

colleague. "So you said we won't be releasing the results of this?"

"No," replied Kovac. "Dexter and the others have no idea how far we've progressed."

"If they knew about this," said the other man, "they'd probably think twice about shutting us down."

"It's more likely they'd be much more worried about defection," Kovac corrected him. "Keeping Dexter and the others in the dark makes it more likely that we'll get away with all our research data. We can then restart the project somewhere else."

"Somewhere else?

"I've changed my employers before, Doctor Lawrence," replied Kovac. "We've already had offers from the Russians and China, even the Middle East. We might even end up with a wealthy private backer, rather than a government. Wherever we go, the others will eventually be there too."

"But they're nowhere near ready yet," said Lawrence.

"Perhaps," Kovac replied, "but you remember what Kane was like when he first came to us? That girl has significant abilities and eventually she might be at Kane's level. Still, I'll admit that none of the other ones we've tested here has been anywhere near as impressive. Not like the ones Kane's been in contact with telepathically. Did you know he can connect with others, anywhere in the world? Imagine them working together."

"Are we ready to proceed, Doctor?"

A young man, with shoulder-length dirty blonde hair swept back from his face was standing in the doorway. Max shuddered as he recognized the younger version of Kane.

"Yes," said Kovac, "bring him in."

Kane stepped back into the corridor then returned pushing a gurney on which lay a blindfolded man, who had tape covering his mouth. Kane and Lawrence lifted the seemingly unconscious man from the gurney and tied him to the chair in the centre of the room, his hands and arms bound behind his back.

Fifteen feet in front of him, Kane stood perfectly still, staring at the man with an expression indicating intense concentration. At first, nothing happened, but then it appeared that the man in the chair was now awake and in considerable discomfort. His body seemed to be steadily consumed by tremors and his head began violently shaking from side to side. The man was obviously in excruciating pain. Blood began to trickle first from the man's nose, then from his ears, and even from beneath his blindfold—the man's eyes were clearly bulging and bleeding too. Then abruptly it was all over. The man's head slumped to his chest, his shirt covered in blood.

"Very impressive, Kane," said Kovac, clapping his hands. "Very impressive."

"Thank you, Doctor," Kane replied.

"Take him away," said Kovac. "Get the girl ready for the lab procedure and get me an update from Connor about that boy."

Kovac left the room, leaving Kane and Lawrence to untie the unfortunate man, put him back on the gurney, and wheel him out of the room. Max felt sick to his stomach at what he'd witnessed. He suspected Kane possessed some sort of mental ability, but this went far beyond what Max had experienced at the police station or anything that Deanna had told him about. It looked as if Kane had killed the man, just with the power of his mind.

When he was sure it was safe, Max crept out from behind the filing cabinets. He cautiously went over to the doorway and peered out into the empty corridor. He crept along the passage until he reached another room, which resembled a hospital. Twelve beds were positioned around the perimeter, all connected by wires and cables to various forms of computer equipment or medical devices. All but two of the beds were empty.

On the nearest one lay the man Max had witnessed being subjected to Kane's mental assault. He looked in pretty bad shape, with a number of thin wires leading from adjacent medical machinery to his left arm and other areas of his upper body. His right arm was connected to a drip and a machine was monitoring his evidently weak vital signs. On the farthest bed lay a young woman with short-cropped green hair, who looked to be asleep, or more likely sedated. Her face was turned away from him, but Max shuddered when he realized it had to be Deanna Hastings.

He was about to walk over to verify the woman's identity when Max felt his knees buckle and he collapsed to the floor. He tried in vain to stand. He felt as if his head was going to split open from the incredible pressure and started to black out. Kane was standing over him, concentrating intensely, his pale blue eyes locked on Max's own.

"You're Dexter's kid, aren't you," he sneered, as Max felt the pressure at his temples and forehead ease. "Evans said you were here somewhere."

He flashed a thin smile that made Max's skin crawl.

"We've never met before, have we?" Kane asked. "I've met your father a few times, but it's odd how you seem so familiar. Maybe I should take a quick look at your brain?"

Max could feel the uncomfortable sensation returning as Kane fixed him with an intense stare. In a matter of seconds, Kane would be inside his thoughts and would surely discover that David Dexter wasn't quite what, or rather who, he appeared to be.

"Kane," came Kovac's voice from the overhead speaker. "Is the girl ready?"

"Yes, Doctor," Kane responded, his expression returning to normal. "I'll be right there. I have the Dexter boy too."

"Bring him to me," said Kovac.

"On my way," replied Kane then turned to Max. "You're coming with me."

"What . . . what are you doing with those people?" Max asked, hardly able to speak, as Kane grabbed his arm and roughly escorted him from the room.

"Doctor Kovac still has some plans for the girl," said Kane with that same unnerving smile that Max had experienced in the future, "but the man's scheduled to leave. The operation's winding down, after all. They'll be given the amnesia drug, so that they'll forget their experience. We'll dump them in one of the city parks, or some other remote place, as usual. We'd prefer to release the man alive, but he may well be dead when the authorities find him."

Kane never relaxed his grip as he pulled Max along. Max found himself wondering how long Kane had been working with Kovac.

"When I was around five or six, I started hearing voices in my head, then realized I could actually read people's thoughts."

Max suddenly felt as if a thousand miniature snakes were slithering around inside his brain. He glanced over at Kane, who wore a cruel smile. He was talking to Max telepathically.

"Soon I learned that I could hurt people, but wasn't always able to control my power. I accidentally killed a boy at a park when we got into a fight, although fortunately no one suspected the true cause of his death. After his arrival from Europe, Doctor Kovac took me to a military base in Nevada, before they set up the operation here."

Now Max understood what had happened to him when he'd met Kane at the police station. Kane had been probing his mind, just as Deanna had said. Max still had no recollection of just how long he'd been unconscious in the interview room.

"I've been working on techniques to initiate heart attacks and other causes of death that are virtually impossible to pinpoint as murder. Eventually Doctor Kovac plans to send me on covert missions all over the world."

"Stop it, Kane."

Kovac had stepped out into the corridor just ahead of them.

"Use verbal communication," he told Kane. "His brain needs to be free of distortions if he's going to be of any use to me."

He then turned his attention to Max, who shuddered as he saw the interior of the room behind Kovac. It was the laboratory he'd seen in his visions from David's memories.

"So David," Kovac said as Kane ushered Max into the lab. "Doctor Evans told me you'd paid us a visit. And with a private detective, no less."

"Is it that guy who's been snooping around about the missing person cases?" Kane asked him.

"Yes, Carrington," confirmed Kovac. "If Connor and Drake have finished, see what else you can get out of him. You can use him for practice, if you like?"

"Thank you," said Kane, grinning. "I'll get the girl first and send her over."

He turned to head back down the corridor, closing the laboratory door behind him.

CHAPTER FOURTEEN
BEYOND THE VEIL

LAWRENCE AND EVANS were working in the laboratory, which was filled with banks of computers, a variety of monitors and numerous consoles in different shapes and sizes. Almost filling one wall was a glass panel resembling a big screen TV. In front of it was a long narrow table, with an attached metal tray, filled with an assortment of surgical instruments. More ominously, at one end of the long table, on the end of an extendable mechanical arm attached to the floor, was a mysterious black circular object, from which wires and cables trailed down.

"Your father's agency helped pay for all this," said Kovac. "He also secured us the resources we needed to not only abduct the subjects we needed for experiments, but also to keep it all quiet."

"But how could he ever do such a thing?" Max demanded.

"This is a military program, David," replied Kovac, matter-of-factly, with a dismissive sweep of his hand. "The ends always justify the means as far as the generals are concerned, no matter what it costs or how many people get hurt."

"But surely someone would talk?" said Max. "You can't keep something like this a secret."

Kovac simply smiled.

"We've perfected drugs which create what you might term selective amnesia in the minds of those that we release back onto the street," he explained. "Once we're done with them, we leave them in a quieter part of the city in the middle of the night, in a deserted park perhaps, or even in a rural area. They're temporarily confused, but soon recover. They go back to their daily lives, although they have no memory of ever having been here. Admittedly, sometimes people die, but if they have families and friends, an elaborate cover story is always developed. Ah, here she is."

Connor and Drake entered the laboratory, pushing a gurney on which lay the unconscious Deanna Hastings.

"We have high hopes for this one," Kovac explained. "Her test results were very impressive yesterday. We would never have heard about her at all, if she hadn't alerted us to her presence. Most psychics are very reserved about their unique talent, keeping a low profile. But this one had taken to doing readings for her friends at parties at the university. All strictly private affairs of course, but to us, nothing stays private for long."

Max watched as Connor and Drake left the room. Lawrence and Evans gently lifted Deanna from the gurney onto what Max could only assume was an operating table. Deanna appeared to revive a little as Lawrence tightly secured her with sturdy restraints. Meanwhile, Evans busily attached the cables leading from the circular device into a wide console filled with switches and dials. Once she'd made all the connections, she positioned the mechanical arm, then placed the round device over the top of Deanna's head. Lawrence then took over, making a few adjustments to the device itself and the huge screen behind the operating table became active, although it remained blank.

"We've made significant progress with our research into psychics," said Kovac. "You met Kane, of course."

Max grimaced at the recent memory.

"Kane is one of my most successful subjects," Kovac continued, "a star pupil, if you prefer. Since he first came to us, we've been able to channel his ability into a powerful weapon in what we call *Project Mindstorm*. The potential for military operations is almost limitless. Imagine an army composed of men like him, or even what just a handful of such people could achieve against the enemy? It's simply . . ."

Kovac was interrupted by an ear-piercing screech. Deanna screamed again, struggling wildly against her restraints.

"Sedate her!" Kovac ordered.

Lawrence nodded in acknowledgement. Evans reached for a large hypodermic needle lying on the metal tray beside the operating table. Max shuddered as she injected something into the lower arm of Deanna, who then lay quiet.

"I've always been fascinated by near-death experiences," said Kovac, as if nothing had happened. "I have a theory that if we can tap into a person's memories at that crucial point, especially someone with psychic abilities, their mental powers will be almost limitless. Some of our test subjects have had very strong links to what some people refer to as the other side. This machine is able to access that surreal world, through the mind of the patient. We've actually viewed tantalizing glimpses of what may lie beyond the veil of death, right on that screen on the wall. We've never really been able to learn as much as we'd like, but we made a crucial breakthrough last month. I only needed one more live subject, but when your father announced that he was cutting off the funding, all my work was in jeopardy."

Max noticed that the huge screen was no longer blank. Disjointed images began flashing across the surface of the glass. Max quickly realized that he was viewing images from Deanna's subconscious mind. He saw a little girl, no more than five or six years old, running through a field, then a man and woman that Max presumed were Deanna's parents. Then there was the little girl again, this time cradling a small puppy in her arms. The picture soon shifted to scenes of her playing with the same dog when it was older. Other episodes from Deanna's childhood and adolescence flashed by in quick succession, before ones that had clearly taken place more recently at the university with her student friends. Then without warning, the screen began to show something else entirely.

Max watched in astonishment as swirling shapes flickered across the screen. At first, they resembled mere wisps of a light gray smoke, but then Max was convinced some were almost human or animal in appearance. He couldn't tear his gaze away from the screen, sure that he was somehow watching spirits inhabiting another plane of existence. Then a teenage Deanna was once again displayed, but she wasn't alone. She was seated on a bench beside a bus stop and behind her stood an elderly woman wearing clothes that Max imagined would have been fashionable over an hundred years earlier. Pinned to the woman's pale blue blouse was a golden brooch, which looked to be in the shape of a flower, although Max couldn't be sure. The woman was short in stature and quite heavyset, with brilliant white hair. She carefully placed a hand on Deanna's shoulder. Deanna turned her head towards the woman, who smiled reassuringly, then gave a single nod.

Suddenly, on the operating table the unconscious Deanna looked to be having a seizure. Her back arched repeatedly and her limbs twitched violently in spasms of pain.

"What's going on?" Kovac demanded.

"We're losing her!" exclaimed Lawrence.

Of course you are, Max thought.

He began to understand what the presence of the old woman on the screen truly signified. Deanna's great-grandmother was literally standing squarely behind Deanna in her struggle, helping Deanna to resist the penetration of her innermost mind. It was almost as if Deanna was prepared to sacrifice her life rather than give up her secrets. Lawrence and Evans were doing their best to save Deanna, but they looked to be fighting a losing battle. Yet Max knew that she couldn't die, since she had to be alive in the future to send him back. Or did she?

He found himself wondering whether the previous sequence of events had now altered for Deanna too. But what would happen if Deanna died? What if he was trapped in the past? A monitor next to the operating table didn't exactly indicate that Deanna had slipped away, but the pattern it displayed was terrifyingly close to a flat line. Then to Max's relief, Deanna's condition seemed to stabilize. On the monitor, her vital signs returned to something approaching normal, but the enormous screen on the wall was now blank.

"There's too much resistance," said Lawrence, reaching for the device placed over Deanna's head. "I'll try a higher setting."

"That won't be necessary," said Kovac, shaking his head. "I don't think she's going to be any use to us after all."

Lawrence nodded. He removed the circular device then quickly unfastened the straps binding Deanna to the table. He and Evans then eased Deanna's almost comatose body onto the gurney.

"Your father was only here this morning," Kovac told Max, "finalizing the arrangements to close everything down. To think that all I needed was one more live subject and your father was going to deny me that. But then you arrived here. It's too good an opportunity to ignore, don't you agree? A means to complete my research, while having my revenge against the high and mighty Jonathan Dexter. Secure him."

Evans and Lawrence grabbed Max, pinning his

arms behind his back.

"You'll never get away with this!" Max yelled, struggling in vain as they pulled him towards the operating table.

"Really?" said Kovac. "Do you seriously think another missing person will be noticed? Even if your father does suspect that I'm somehow connected to your imminent demise, he can hardly go to the police now, can he? Not without drawing attention to his own involvement. On the contrary, David, I will most certainly get away with it."

CHAPTER FIFTEEN
ALL IN THE MIND

KOVAC AND LAWRENCE roughly heaved Max onto the table then held him in place while Evans fastened Max's wrists into the security restraints. Max coughed and spluttered when Lawrence finally let him go, before Evans placed surgical tape over Max's mouth.

"Tell Connor to use Castlegate Park this time," Kovac told Evans, "if they're going to be dumping the girl in the daylight. They should probably leave the man in the woods. And get Kane back in here."

"I'll administer the amnesia drug first," said Evans. "It needs some time to take effect."

She left the laboratory, pushing the gurney, while Kovac and Lawrence turned their attention to the instrument panels. At Max's shoulder was the shallow metal tray filled with surgical instruments, including a lengthy needle similar to the one that he'd seen used on Deanna only moments earlier. Beside the tray hung the black machine, its collection of cables still attached to the nearby console. The shiny black outer surface had a series of four lights in blue, red, yellow, and green, above corresponding switches. There was also a small dial, which Max assumed operated the device's power level. He figured this was what Lawrence had been reaching for, to change the setting of the probe into Deanna's brain.

It seemed that no matter what Max tried to do, his mission was doomed to failure. He could tinker with the chain of events, but David still appeared destined to die, just at a different time, as a result of Kovac's experiments. Even if by some miracle Max survived the upcoming procedure, by now he'd seen far too much. He knew that there was no chance of Kovac allowing him to leave the waterfront alive. What if Max had influenced Deanna's fate as well? He'd always assumed that she'd survive, so that she could send him back in the first place. Yet Deanna had looked to be in a very bad way when they'd taken her out of the laboratory. And what about Carrington? Before Max had traveled back into the past, the detective had probably never been anywhere near the waterfront. Now it looked as if he might even be killed.

Kane had returned and approached the table, checking the restraints, apparently satisfied that Max was securely fastened down. Kovac reached for the tape covering Max's mouth and tore it away with a sharp tug.

"What are you going to do?" Max demanded, his

voice shaking.

"Basically, you'll die," Kovac explained with another cruel smile, "very slowly, under controlled conditions, so that we can observe any near-death experience that you might have. Put him under, Doctor Lawrence. Just a little at first."

Before Max could protest, Lawrence quickly swabbed his upper arm and injected him with the needle. The effect of the drug was almost instantaneous. Max first felt his arms and legs become limp, then he began to lose consciousness, but soon imagined himself to be in a long, dark tunnel. A brilliant white light was shining at the far end and although Max couldn't feel his feet touching the ground, he was being pulled steadily towards the brightness. Then abruptly the tunnel and light vanished and Max could hardly believe what he was seeing. He was floating in the air close to the laboratory ceiling, looking down at David Dexter's body lying on the operating table. He could clearly hear Kovac and the others talking about the procedure that they were performing.

On the wall, scenes were playing out on the big screen involving Christmas gifts, a concert including a piano performance, a skiing trip, and a tropical vacation. These were obviously among David's strongest memories. Abruptly, David's recollections were replaced by images from Max's own life. He saw his home, his school, his friends, and his dad, pictured on the screen in rapid succession. Both Deanna Hastings and John Carrington, in their older incarnations, also appeared fleetingly. The image on the screen shifted again. It now showed the tall gravestone dedicated to Jonathan Dexter, complete with the dates of his birth and future death, along with the smaller grave belonging to David. Max saw himself standing beside Jonathan Dexter's memorial. In the laboratory beneath him, Kovac and the others were all staring at the screen in utter amazement.

"What the hell is this?" Kovac demanded. "What's going on?"

"I'm not sure," said Lawrence, checking the controls on the machine attached to Max's head.

"Administer the final dose," Kovac ordered. "We'll soon see what this is all about."

Suddenly, Max was forced back into David's body.

"Are the restraints tight enough?" Kovac asked.

"Yes, of course they are," replied Lawrence. "I told you, I know what I'm doing."

"Now keep still, David, this won't hurt a bit."

Yet the twisted smile on Kovac's face told a far different story. Max struggled against the bonds securing him to the operating table as Kovac's hand moved closer. Max clearly saw the hypodermic, the needle now only inches from his eye. Kane grinned as Max emitted a scream that he was certain no one would ever hear.

"Wait!" Kane exclaimed. "There's something very odd going on here. When I first connected with him, it was as if there was another presence in his mind. It wasn't like anything I'd ever experienced before."

"Can you sense the same thing now?" Kovac asked him.

"I think I can," Kane replied. "Let me try and probe a little deeper."

His brow furrowed in intense concentration, Kane looked deeply into Max's face then suddenly his eyes widened in astonishment.

"This is absolutely incredible," he declared. "The boy is . . ."

"Doctor Kovac!" exclaimed Evans, as she burst into the lab. "The police are coming!"

"The police?"

"We saw them with the cameras just off the main road," Evans replied. "There must be six or seven cars and vans heading here."

"What the hell are they doing here?" demanded Kovac.

"That detective," Kane sneered. "He must have tipped them off when he got here, before we captured him and the boy."

"They'll be here in less than ten minutes," said Evans.

"We have to destroy everything!" Lawrence declared.

He went over to the nearest console and began flicking switches and turning dials, then began frantically typing on one of the computer keyboards.

"There's no time," barked Kovac. "Just get the boy out, he can't be found here. Give him the other shot."

Lawrence quickly grabbed another hypodermic from the tray and injected the needle into Max's arm. Almost instantly, Max felt himself reviving from his drowsiness.

"Is that detective still alive?" Kovac asked.

"I don't know," replied Evans. "They had him over at the north shed, but Connor and Drake have already left for the city with the girl."

"Lawrence," Kovac ordered, "go with her and destroy those file folders and disks in the other room. Hurry!"

Evans and Lawrence rushed from the lab, leaving the door wide open in their haste to get away.

"You can't just shut this down," Kane protested. "Not when we're this close."

"We don't have a choice," replied Kovac as he continued whatever Lawrence had been doing at the keyboard and adjacent consoles. "We can't let the police find all this."

"But we were so close," said Kane.

"You know we have copies of all the research and records safely hidden," Kovac reminded him. "We'll be able to start again, eventually, once all this blows over."

"But when will that be?" demanded Kane, in exasperation. "We only needed one more session for me to maximize my power. You said so yourself, only yesterday."

"I know, I know," said Kovac, as he returned to the table and quickly unfastened Max's restraints.

"You're worried I'll get too powerful. That's it, isn't it?" said Kane. "You never wanted me to reach my full potential, did you?"

"How can you say that?" Kovac shot back. "You know it's all been about you."

"Yeah, I'm like a son to you," said Kane sarcastically. "You said that yesterday as well."

"Kane, we really don't have time for this right now."

While they argued back and forth, Max saw his chance. He reached over to the shallow tray and seized the needle that had been destined for his eye, plunging it into the hand of an astonished Kovac.

"My god," the doctor gasped.

Kovac briefly staggered around then collapsed.

Before Kane could react, Max shoved the heavy mechanical arm at him. Kane was hit in the head, stumbling backward against the computer monitors, then dropped to the floor. The metal arm hit the main screen, shattering it and showering Kane in glass.

Max leapt from the table and raced from the lab, but just before he reached the door, he felt his knees start to buckle. Glancing over his shoulder, Max saw Kane getting to his feet, his face covered in blood. Max could feel the pressure building inside his head as Kane once more attempted to enter his mind. Max managed to stagger out into the corridor where the pain in his head eased. As he raced along the passage, Max hoped that Kane had a limited range with his mental powers.

When Max got back to the steel building, he sprinted for the entrance. Pausing to look outside, he immediately noticed that the white van was missing. He also noted the shed, where Evans had mentioned that Carrington was being kept.

CHAPTER SIXTEEN
A KIND OF JUSTICE

ONE OF THE men Max had seen earlier with Connor and Drake was just stepping out of one of the wooden buildings. Max noted the pistol in a holster on the man's belt. He was scanning the surroundings and looked to be talking on a small radio. Max assumed he was getting instructions from either Lawrence or Evans, now that Kovac was incapacitated. Max watched as the man finished his conversation and went back inside. Max raced over and stood flat against the wall beside the entrance. He could hear voices inside the building.

"So what did she say?"

"We have to get moving, right now."

"What about him?"

"We take him with us. He knows too much, but we can't kill him here."

"So we dump him in the woods?"

"Yeah, let's get the car."

Max heard the sound of a door opening then slamming shut. After watching the men run over to the steel building, Max crept inside the shed. He saw Carrington tied to a chair and hurried over.

"Where the hell did you come from?" said Carrington.

His face was covered in bruises. He also had two black eyes and looked to be missing several teeth.

"Long story," Max replied as he struggled to untie the rope securing Carrington to the chair. "But the cops are on their way. Are you okay? What did they do to you?"

"They beat me up, asked me a lot of questions," replied Carrington. "They plan to kill me for sure. Hurry up with those ropes. Those guys will be back any minute."

"I don't think so," said Max, as he finally undid the rope.

Looking out the window, he saw a car that had been blocked by a police van.

"It looks like they've already got them. You called on that radio when we got here, didn't you?

"Yeah," Carrington confirmed, forcing a smile as Max helped him to his feet. "What about you? Where did you go?"

As they made their way to the entrance, Max told Carrington everything that had happened. For the moment, at least, he didn't mention Kane in great detail, or what he'd witnessed during Deanna's procedure. Max wasn't sure if Carrington would believe him. In this time period at least, the detective had never indicated that he knew about the exact nature of Kovac's work. Carrington didn't seem in the least bit surprised at Max's revelations.

"Yeah," he said, "they've probably been abducting people for years and bringing them here for experiments."

"There were only two people here," Max told him. "They're dumping them in Castlegate Park. I'll bet they used that van."

"What van?"

"There was a van here when we arrived," Max explained. "It had a company name on the side, Richardson's something or other, I don't remember exactly."

"Did you get the license plate?" asked Carrington.

"No," Max replied. "I never got close enough."

"Don't worry," said Carrington. "I'll tell the guys and they can watch for the van. We'll get them."

Standing in the doorway, they saw that a number of police vehicles had arrived. Officers were fanning out among the various buildings. The men who'd been guarding Carrington were already being questioned.

"The police will probably want to talk to you," said Carrington.

"What?" Max exclaimed.

"I know I said I'd try and keep your dad and you out of this," said Carrington, "but since you're here, it's going to be pretty hard to explain. I'll do my best, no promises. Wait here while I go and talk to them."

He walked over to the group of police officers supervising the operation. Max watched as Evans and Lawrence were escorted outside. Kovac was barely able to walk. He was supported by two police officers as he and the others were taken to one of the cars. There was no sign of Kane.

Max had to admit that the police might eventually track down Connor and Drake and tie them to the operation. But that might be too late to help Deanna, who was Max's only ticket back to his own time. He had no idea if she'd still be alive when someone found her. Max edged toward where Carrington's truck was parked then ran, not stopping until he reached the far end of the waterfront.

Catching his breath, Max wondered if he'd managed to "put things right". Kovac and his team were in police custody and Jonathan Dexter had cancelled the project. And yet Max remembered that Carrington had told him in the future that the operation was probably still going on. How was that possible if Max had changed how events unfolded?

Max was puzzled that he couldn't precisely recall Carrington's face. He felt disoriented and wondered what he was doing down by the waterfront. He vaguely remembered getting ready for his father's dinner party, then traveling in a limousine, but after that, his mind was just a blank. Wasn't he supposed to be practicing for the piano contest? He felt dizzy and stepped out into the street, only to jerk back sharply when a passing car almost collided with him, speeding away with a loud and lengthy bleat of its horn.

Max shook his head. He'd been drifting into David's thoughts and wondered if this was because he'd altered the timeline. Max concentrated as hard as he could. He could now picture Carrington's face both in this era and in the future, as well as aspects from his real life. Yet some of his memories were becoming increasingly sketchy. He shuddered when he considered the passing car, speculating that David might still be fated to die, if not in an experiment, then as the result of a car accident. Max knew that he had no time to lose. And the only person who could send him back to his own time was about to be dumped in Castlegate Park.

CHAPTER SEVENTEEN
PRESENT LIFE PROGRESSION

THE PARK WASN'T that far from the waterfront. As he ran along the city streets, Max wondered how he was going to find Deanna. He might as well be looking for a miniscule needle in a gigantic haystack.

However, once he reached the park, Max decided that if Deanna had been abandoned, unconscious, in the park, she wasn't going to have been left in plain view. If someone were driving a vehicle in order to dump a body, then make a quick getaway, the drop off point would have to be near the roadway that wound through the park.

Then he saw the *Richardson's Heating and Refrigeration* van emerging from a dirt track that led into the trees. The van quickly drove away and Max hurried over to the entrance of the track.

At first he couldn't see anything untoward as he

peered into the bushes, then he saw something moving in the tangled undergrowth. He immediately recognized Deanna's green hair as she struggled to stand up.

Max hurried over to her.

"Hey," he said. "Are you okay? What happened to you?"

Max had decided that he would innocently pose as a well-meaning passerby at first. He'd then try and explain his fantastic story to Deanna once the opportunity presented itself.

"What?" Deanna mumbled, as she struggled to sit up. "Where am I?"

"Castlegate Park," said Max. "Are you hurt?"

"Where am I?" Deanna asked again, looking extremely confused.

Max had never seen the young Deanna this close. Apart from the colour of her hair, Max was struck by how much she resembled the older person that he'd met in the future. Her brown eyes were a little dull, probably as a result of the amnesia drug, but Max felt that he'd have recognized her anywhere. He knew that Deanna would probably have no recollection of how she'd arrived at the park. However, he was gambling that the amnesia drug would normally take a while to work. Max hoped that by reviving her earlier than may have happened in the previous reality, he'd have a better chance of helping Deanna piece her memories back together.

"Come on," he said, as he helped Deanna to stand. "Let's get you out of these bushes for a start."

They walked over to the lakeshore and sat down on the bench close to where Max had first talked to John

Carrington in the future. At first, Deanna simply stared ahead while she collected her thoughts.

"So who are you, kid?" she eventually asked. "Do I know you?"

"My name's David," said Max. "Do you remember anything unusual about the last few days?"

"Not especially," Deanna replied, shaking her head. "I know that I was over at a friend's place last night."

"I don't think that was last night," Max said, grimly. "You probably have no memory of the last three or four days."

"What do you mean?" asked Deanna.

"You were kidnapped," Max told her. "They took you to a laboratory and performed experiments on you. They were investigating your psychic abilities."

Deanna stared at him open mouthed, then quickly turned her head to face the lake.

"I don't know what you're talking about," she said, defensively.

"They found out about your skills because of the readings you were doing for your friends," Max continued. "Once the scientists had finished with you, they gave you some sort of drug to make you forget everything, before they left you in the park. Please try to think. Do you remember anything, anything at all?"

"Oh my God," said Deanna, appearing distressed, "now I *do* remember. I was on my way home from my friend's apartment. It was getting dark, but wasn't that late. I heard footsteps, then without warning I was grabbed from behind and something was placed over my nose and mouth."

"Do you recall anything else?" Max asked her.

"Anything about a laboratory?"

"Yes, I mean, no," Deanna stammered. "I mean, I'm not sure. What the heck did they do to me?"

Max attempted to describe what he knew of the work that was performed at the facility, including what he'd witnessed when Deanna had been brought into the laboratory on the gurney. He was about to tell her what he'd seen on the huge screen, when Deanna stopped him.

"Wait a second," she said. "What's your connection to all this?"

"Let's get you home first," replied Max. "I'll do my best to explain."

Fortunately, Deanna's apartment wasn't too far from the park. She lived on the second floor and occasionally had to lean on Max for support as they climbed the stairs.

When they reached the door, Max waited patiently as Deanna fumbled for her keys, then followed her into the apartment.

"Sorry about the mess," she apologized. "My roommate's away this week and I promised to tidy up before she gets back. Do want a drink of something?"

"Sure," said Max.

Deanna headed into the kitchen while Max scanned his surroundings. Most of the walls of the apartment were decorated with posters of the musical stars and movie actors of the time. In the far corner stood a medium sized houseplant that looked in desperate need of water. In the centre of the room were two well-worn armchairs covered in widely differing fabrics, and several books, magazines and even a few items of clothing were scattered across the solitary couch. The coffee table bore several circular stains, two empty glasses, and a mug half full of what looked like cold tea.

"Sorry," said Deanna as she emerged from the kitchen, "there's nothing to drink in the fridge."

"No problem," Max replied.

He took a deep breath.

"This is going to sound completely crazy," he said, "but please hear me out. My real name is Max. Twenty years from now, you sent me back here into the life of a boy called David Dexter."

"Is this some kind of joke?" Deanna exclaimed, angrily. "Are you playing some sort of stupid prank here or what? Did someone put you up to this?"

"I know it's hard to believe, even for you," said Max, "but it's completely true. I have to admit that I would never have believed it myself. You put me under hypnosis and I appeared in this time period, occupying someone else's body and . . ."

"Okay," Deanna stopped him, "I'm not sure what you're trying to pull here—"

"But you have to believe me!" Max interrupted her. "You're my only chance to get back."

"Get out!" yelled Deanna. "Just get out!"

"I know how you first learned that you were a psychic," Max exclaimed in desperation. "You were on your way home from school, waiting for a bus. An elderly woman dressed in old-fashioned clothes sat down on the end of the bench and smiled at you. She knew your name, said that you had a special gift, and told you that she was your great-grandmother."

"How could you possibly know that?" Deanna demanded, looking utterly bewildered.

"Because you told me!" Max declared defiantly.

"Twenty years from now. I know it sounds insane, but you have to believe me. Your great-grandmother appears to you as a kindly old woman. She isn't very tall and has white hair. She wears a light blue blouse and a tiny gold brooch shaped like a flower. I saw her on the screen."

"You saw her *where*?" said Deanna.

"She appeared on the screen in the lab," said Max. "The doctors said that you were offering too much resistance. They even thought that you were going to die. But when I saw that old lady on the screen, I knew that you weren't fighting alone."

Tears began streaming down Deanna's face. She mumbled something to excuse herself, then dashed into the kitchen. Max heard her sobbing uncontrollably and knew that he'd finally got through to her. He just hoped that it would be enough to persuade her to help him.

Momentarily, Deanna returned from the kitchen.

"Okay," she said. "Max, or David, or whatever your real name is. Let's sit down, shall we?"

Deanna walked over to the couch, cleared away the clutter and invited Max to take a seat. She wiped the last of the tears from her eyes, then sat down at the opposite end of the couch.

"There's a way I can find out if you're on the level," she said. "Do you mind?"

"What do you need to do?" Max asked her.

Deanna held out her hands, her palms facing upward.

"Take my hands," Deanna instructed him, "and just relax. Breathe deeply and try to clear your mind."

Max did as he was told and placed his hands over

Deanna's. He watched as she closed her eyes and her brow furrowed in intense concentration. In less than a minute, her eyes opened, then widened in astonishment.

"My God!" she gasped. "You're actually telling the truth, aren't you? There really is another person inside you somehow. I never thought I'd see anything like it. But how?"

Max related as quickly as possible everything that had happened. He wasn't sure if he should tell Deanna about the future, since it might affect the timeline in ways that he didn't dare to contemplate. But Max was beyond worrying about that now. Deanna listened intently to everything that he had to say, only stopping him occasionally to clarify one point or another.

"And you say," she asked, when Max had finished, "that you sometimes feel that you're going to be completely submerged in David's memories?"

"I do," Max confirmed. "It's been hard to suppress them and remember who I really am."

"Yes," Deanna nodded. "It may only be a matter of time before you and David eventually become one."

"You don't have to tell *me* that," said Max. "I need to get back."

"But is it even possible?" Deanna said, in exasperation. "I mean, past lives are one thing, but what you're talking about is entirely different."

"I know," Max agreed, "but you're the only one who can help me. You know what past life regression is, right? This would be the same thing in reverse, wouldn't it?"

"I don't know," said Deanna, shaking her head.

"What if something goes wrong?"

"Trust me," Max said. "You're an expert, or at least you will be, twenty years from now."

"But I haven't even tried sending anyone into their past life yet," Deanna protested, "let alone what you're proposing."

"It's my only chance," Max said. "I don't know how much longer I can hold back these thoughts. I could be trapped here forever or even disappear altogether."

"Okay," said Deanna with a shrug, then took a deep breath. "Let's give this a try. Close your eyes and breathe deeply."

Max did as she asked and he soon began to feel comfortable, just as he had done in the future.

"Keep breathing deeply," said Deanna. "Just relax, deep breaths."

Her voice soon began to fade away, until eventually it was completely gone.

CHAPTER EIGHTEEN
REVISIONS

MAX HAD EXPECTED to find himself back in Deanna's house in his own time. Instead he felt a warm breeze on his face and when he opened he eyes, he could hardly believe what he saw. He was in the cemetery, after he and Jeff had bought pizza. Across the road, he could see Jeff and his grandmother, Mrs. McNally, tending the flowers at the grave and Max recalled how he'd chosen to allow them a few moments of privacy.

Max felt dizzy and disoriented. He rested his hand on a nearby gravestone to steady himself but didn't experience any of the visions that had previously flooded his mind. Then he saw two people a little further up the road close to a parked car.

Max immediately recognized Vanessa Dexter. The man standing with her at the graveside Max estimated to be in his mid-thirties. As he cautiously approached the gravesite, Max noted that it was covered in fresh flowers and wreaths. The memorial to Jonathan Dexter was absent, along with the smaller gravestone. When he got closer, to his astonishment, Max recognized that the man was clearly an older David Dexter. While David and his mother stood in respectful silence for a few moments, Max edged as close as he dared. Mrs. Dexter turned away from the grave and started back toward the car. David noticed Max watching them and eyed him curiously.

"Can I help you?" he said.

"No," said Max then thinking quickly, added, "My dad used to talk about Mr. Dexter. He helped a lot of people."

"Have we met somewhere?" David asked, with a puzzled expression on his face as he took a few steps closer. "You seem very familiar."

"I don't think so," Max replied. "I just wanted to pay my respects, that's all."

"Well, thank you," said David, politely, extending his hand for Max to shake. "It was nice of you to stop by."

Max reached out to grab David Dexter's outstretched hand. When their palms touched, Max experienced a flood of images from his experiences in David's life, traveling at incredible speed across his mind. Max let go of David's hand and took a step backwards, staggering slightly as he did so.

"Are you all right?" David asked.

"Yes, yes thanks," said Max, haltingly.

"Good," said David with a smile. "Well, it was nice of you to stop by."

Max watched as David returned to the car, which then drove off through the cemetery gates.

"You okay, Max?"

Max was startled as he turned around to see Jeff and his grandmother standing there.

"You don't look so good," said Jeff.

"I'm okay," Max replied, although he did feel incredibly confused.

"Who was that guy?" Jeff asked him.

"What?" said Max. "Oh, just someone my dad used to talk about, his son anyway, visiting the grave. Just wanted to say hi, you know."

"Are you sure you're okay, Max?" asked Mrs. McNally, with an expression of concern.

"Yeah, I think so," said Max, forcing a smile.

"You going to be okay for the game?" Jeff asked him. "You've never missed one yet."

Max remembered he was supposed to be playing third base that afternoon, but he knew he couldn't be at the game. With his thoughts still reeling, he had to get home, even if he couldn't tell Jeff the truth.

"You certainly do look a little pale, Max," remarked Mrs. McNally.

"Maybe you should just go home?" Jeff suggested. "I'll get someone to fill in on third, no big deal."

"You might be right," said Max.

He was still trying to wrap his head around how the conversation was virtually the same as before. It was so weird.

"Sorry about the game."

"No problem," said Jeff. "Jason and the others will be there for sure. Are you sure you're going be all right?"

"Yeah," Max nodded. "You'd better get going or you'll miss everyone."

"Well, we're about done here," said Mrs. McNally. "You go with Max, Jeff. Uncle Bill said he'd be here at 1.30 to take me home anyway."

"You sure, Grandma?"

"Yes, I'm sure," replied Mrs. McNally. "You go ahead."

Jeff gave his grandmother a peck on the cheek and he and Max made their way out of the cemetery.

Max hardly paid any attention to what Jeff was saying as they walked, responding just enough to keep the conversation going. Max was still finding the whole bizarre situation so hard to believe. The last thing he remembered from his own time was being in Deanna's house before she'd sent him back into what had been David's life. Had he now returned to where it had all began, before any of what he'd experienced had happened? Had he now never even met Deanna to set the whole process in motion? If he hadn't, how could he have traveled back into David's life and saved him from being killed? After all, he'd just met David, who was older, but very much alive. And what about Carrington? What had happened to him? The entire situation was mind boggling, to say the least.

The lights changed at the intersection and they crossed the road. Max noted the empty bench beside the nearby bus stop. There was no boy in a black shirt and jeans, with a thick mop of dark hair. David had now never died young and been the catalyst for Max's incredible experience.

"You sure you're okay?" asked Jeff. "You seem

pretty spaced out."

"Yeah, sorry," Max replied. "Just tired, I guess."

For the rest of the walk home, Max did his best to participate in the conversation.

"So," said Jeff, as they arrived at the corner of the street where Max lived, "still on for this weekend at Jason's?"

"Jason's?" said Max, before he remembered that this conversation had also happened previously. "Oh yeah, sure. I've been wanting to try that new game."

"Me too," Jeff agreed as he started off down the sidewalk to walk the couple of blocks to his own house.

"Hey look, I'm really sorry about this afternoon," Max called after him.

"No problem," said Jeff. "Like I said, I'll get somebody to cover third. I'll text you tonight."

Max was relieved to see that his dad's truck was missing as he approached the condo. He didn't want to have to engage his dad in conversation just now, not until he got his head together about everything that had happened. He opened the door and hurried inside, closing the door behind him.

Max headed to the kitchen where the newspaper lay open next to a half full cup of coffee. Max quickly checked the paper to see if there was any mention of the Dexter funeral. He turned the pages and found a story entitled *Wealthy Philanthropist Laid to Rest*, complete with a photograph of David and his mother, at what looked to be a very well attended funeral the day before.

Jonathan Dexter, founder and CEO of the Dexter

Foundation, died earlier this week after a short illness. Mr. Dexter at one time held several senior government positions, most notably those connected with science, technology, and defense. He was frequently mentioned as a potential presidential candidate, but resigned at the height of his career to spend more time with his family.

Following his departure from politics, he established the Dexter Foundation and worked tirelessly to make it one of the nation's leading charitable organizations. The Dexter Foundation is involved in many fundraising activities, but has always retained a strong focus on the plight of missing persons and their families. Mr. Dexter leaves a widow, Vanessa, and a son, David, who will replace his father as CEO of the Dexter Foundation.

Everything had changed. Jonathan Dexter had still left politics, but hadn't died in the fire that Carrington had believed was deliberately set to silence the former politician. Vanessa Dexter and David were still alive. They'd obviously been at the cemetery for a private visit after the crowded funeral the previous day.

It seemed to Max that the incident at the waterfront had been covered up somehow. Yet it had still meant the end of Dexter's political career, with a cover story developed to explain his departure from politics. Not surprisingly, there was no mention of Kovac. It seemed highly unlikely to Max that the doctor would have continued working at the university and then recently retired, as reported in the newspaper clipping he'd read at Carrington's office. Max wondered if Kovac had been pensioned off, with his career in tatters, but escaped prosecution, due to the secret nature of the project?

Max wondered what had happened to Carrington too and grabbed the *Yellow Pages* from the kitchen drawer. He was very pleased to see that Carrington was listed under *Investigators* and even had the same office address. Max then thought about Deanna and grabbed the *White Pages*. Sure enough, she was still listed at the same address.

As he put the phone books back in the drawer, Max felt the beginnings of a slight headache. Then to his horror Max realized it was a terrifyingly familiar sensation. He whirled around and instantly recognized Kane standing by the back door near the entrance to the basement steps.

Max ran from the kitchen, banging into the table and smashing the coffee cup on the tiled floor. He got halfway to the front door before his knees gave way and he collapsed onto the rug in front of the fireplace.

"How touching, all your friends living happily ever after."

Max heard the voice in his mind and when he opened his eyes, Kane was standing over him. Max immediately noticed the deep, disfiguring scar running along Kane's right cheek and neck, which Max suspected had been caused by the screen shattering back at the lab. Max could barely speak, as he struggled to cope with the intense pain in his head.

"Where . . . where did you come from?" he murmured. "How . . . how did you know where to find me?"

"I know everything," Kane replied, switching to verbal communication.

He ran his fingers along the scar.

"This is an ever-present reminder of another reality, when I was something else. But you changed all that, didn't you, you and that damned psychic."

"I don't understand," said Max, his voice quivering.

"You don't need to understand anything, Max," Kane sneered. "All you need to do is die. Then the psychic, then Dexter."

Kane began concentrating deeply, the stare from his piercing pale blue eyes growing ever more intense. Max felt his nose starting to bleed. Kane grinned, making his scar appear even more grotesque.

Out of the corner of his eye, Max could see the poker lying on the hearth, tantalizingly just out of reach. Max felt like his head was going to split open as the pressure on his skull dramatically increased. Straining his arm and stretching his fingers, Max finally connected with the handle of the poker.

Kane noticed too late, his concentration broken seconds before Max swung the poker at him. Kane fell back onto the carpet, stunned, but still conscious. The pressure on Max's brain immediately subsided. He struggled to his feet and stumbled out the front door. He knew he had to get as far away from Kane as possible and that only one person could help him now.

CHAPTER NINETEEN
REALITY CHECK

MAX RACED DOWN the street and ran for four blocks. Gasping for breath, he leapt onto the first bus he could find. He needed to find Deanna. Since everything had changed, she wouldn't know who Max was if he showed up on her doorstep. He had no idea how Deanna was going to react. But Max knew he had to take that chance. Deanna might remember him, maybe because of her psychic abilities, but Max had to admit it was a long shot.

Max changed buses just outside downtown. He remembered Deanna's neighbourhood, even if he couldn't recall the exact address. He was hoping that he'd spot something familiar once he arrived in the right part of the city. He'd then have to try and find Deanna's house from memory.

The bus didn't take long to reach the older part of

the city where Deanna lived. Max immediately recognized the mature trees when he got off the bus, but at first he couldn't locate the house. Then as he passed the end of a street, he spotted a black convertible PT Cruiser parked outside a house with a tall hedge. Max ran down the street until he reached Deanna's high wooden gate. Max opened the gate and walked up the path to the front of the house.

Max pressed the bell and a moment later heard footsteps approaching the opposite side of the door.

"Who is it?" said a voice.

"Deanna Hastings?" Max asked.

The door only opened slightly, held back by a chain. Deanna peered out curiously at Max.

"That depends. Who are you?"

"It's me, Max. I really need your help."

"You have the wrong address," said the woman, beginning to close the door.

"No, I don't," said Max, in exasperation, slamming his hand on the door. "You must remember me! Please try and remember!"

"I said," Deanna replied firmly, "you have the wrong address."

"I met David Dexter's ghost!" exclaimed Max, throwing caution to the winds. "Well, I mean, in another timeline anyway. You sent me back into his life! I found you in the park after the experiments, remember?"

"My god, I do remember," said Deanna as she stood in the doorway, looking utterly stunned.

"You do?"

"Yes, yes, I do," she replied, haltingly. "Come in, please."

Max followed Deanna into the house, along the short hallway, past the dark wooden staircase into the sitting room. Everything was the same as Max remembered—the hardwood floor, the Turkish rug, the antique grandfather clock, the framed pictures and the well-stocked bookcases. Deanna walked over to the wide window overlooking the garden at the rear of the house and closed the curtains.

"I always thought this day would come," she told Max as she turned to face him, "although I also didn't expect it to ever arrive. Does that make any sense?"

"No," Max replied, "but then again, not a lot of this makes any sense, does it?"

Deanna began to pace back and forth in front of the window, gently running her slender fingers though her shoulder-length hair.

"I mean, I have these memories of you, or rather you as someone else. It seems like a dream, or something that never happened, but sometimes it's so clear. Years ago, the memories were quite intense but then I managed to suppress them. At times I thought it really had all been imaginary. Yet deep down, I always thought you'd come here. I can't even explain it, it's like—"

"I have to tell you," Max interrupted her, "Kane's coming."

"Kane?" said Deanna, as she stopped pacing and her deep brown eyes scrutinized Max with an intense stare.

"You remember him, right? From the lab? He worked with Kovac."

"I'm not sure," said Deanna, frowning. "Wait a minute. Yes, at the lab, he probed my mind. I haven't thought about him in years. But what do you mean he's coming? Coming here?"

"You have to believe me," Max told her. "At my house, he tried to kill me."

"What?"

"He tried to kill me," Max replied. "Before I got away."

Deanna simply shook her head in disbelief.

"But how does he know who you are, or where you live, for that matter? That's impossible. And how does he know who I am and what my connection is to all this?"

"I know it sounds crazy," said Max, "but he said he's coming for you. I'm not sure if he knows where you live."

"He found you easily enough," Deanna pointed out. "We can assume he'll find me too."

"He mentioned getting David too," Max added. "We have to warn him."

"David Dexter? But he's never going to believe such a bizarre story."

"You're right," said Max. "What are we going to do?"

"I don't know. Give me time to think. Come on, let's get to the car."

As he climbed into Deanna's car, Max's mind was racing, trying to fathom just how Deanna and Kane could even know who he was, since the timeline had utterly changed. Strictly speaking, the sequence of events that had first taken him to Deanna's house had never occurred. He'd also previously met Kane in this time period at the police station and at the coffee shop. But all that had never happened now either, had it?

"So where are we going?" he asked, as he fastened the seatbelt.

"To see David," replied Deanna.

"He was at the cemetery with his family an hour or so ago," Max told her, as the car pulled away. "I met him."

"You actually met him?" said Deanna. "Bet that was weird."

"No kidding," Max agreed. "I mean, I was him, wasn't I, for a while anyway? When I shook his hand, all these images from his life flashed across my mind. His dad's funeral was just the other day and he and his mother were there, paying their respects in private. If they went home, he'll be there by now. Where does he live?"

"His parents moved into a smaller place when Jonathan Dexter became ill," said Deanna. "David and his wife moved into the family home."

"How do you know that?" Max asked her.

"No magic powers, Max," replied Deanna, with a smile. "It was actually in the paper a while ago, when David's dad first became sick and the story caught my eye."

"Is it far from here?"

"No, not far."

"So," Max asked, when they turned onto the main road, "how can you or I remember, if everything's changed?"

"I honestly don't know," said Deanna. "In your case, maybe it's all to do with the sheer strength of your experience. In my case, it might be because of my abilities."

"And that's why Kane can remember everything too?"

"Not sure," Deanna replied, shaking her head. "I've never experienced anything like this before, but I guess it's possible."

"So do you remember me at the park and at your apartment?"

"Yes," said Deanna, "I remember what happened. How you, or rather, David, saved me then I found out that he was possessed by someone else."

"Did he remember anything, once I was gone from his body?"

"No, not really. He was pretty confused," Deanna replied. "My roommate had left me her car when she went out. I took David home, he was still feeling pretty out of it. That's how I know where he lives."

"Have you seen anything of David since then?"

"No," said Deanna. "I never heard from him again. I also forgot about most of what happened over the years, or it felt like a dream."

"Until now."

"That's right," said Deanna, "until you showed up."

"I read a little about David's dad in today's paper," said Max. "He left politics, I would imagine because of what happened at the waterfront."

"Yes, they probably covered it up somehow," agreed Deanna.

"What about Kovac? Before I went back and changed things, he just retired after a successful career at the university."

"I'm not sure what would have happened to him," admitted Deanna. "He most likely wouldn't have worked for the university for long after what happened, if at all."

"So nobody went to jail back then?"

"No," Deanna replied, "I think it all got conveniently forgotten about."

"Maybe Kovac even went to another country? Maybe he's still been doing his experiments somewhere else, all this time. Carrington suggested something like that, I think."

"Not sure, Max," Deanna replied, "but either way, Kane's not been working with him, it seems."

"True. When he turned up my house, he was angry that his life had been ruined. Didn't sound like he'd been on an official project all these years."

As they entered the Dexters' neighbourhood, Max started to recognize his surroundings.

"I think it's down here," said Deanna, as she cautiously drove along the residential streets. "I've got a good memory for places usually. I'm sure I'll recognize the house when I see it. Ah, that's it, I think."

"Yes, it is," Max added. "The house looks pretty much the same."

"Look, Max," she said, as she slowed down. "I'm not sure what we're going to be up against here. I never saw David again and I'm not even sure if he'll remember me. We also shouldn't mention your role in this, okay?"

"So what do we do?" Max asked, as they both got out of the car and walked up the path to the front door.

"If he asks, I'll say you're my nephew and I'm looking after you today. How does that sound?"

"Okay, I guess," Max replied, with a shrug.

"Good, just let me do all the talking."

Deanna rang the doorbell.

"Mr. Dexter?" she said as the door opened.

Max instantly recognized David from the cemetery.

"Yes, who are you?"

"My name is Deanna Hastings. May we come in?"

"What's this about? Wait a minute," said David, his eyes narrowing as he examined Max's face. "You were at the cemetery weren't you?"

"It'll be easier to explain this inside, Mr. Dexter," Deanna continued.

"I don't think so," said David, shaking his head.

He started to close the door, but Deanna used her foot to prevent it from closing.

"It really would be best if we talk inside, David," said Deanna, firmly. "It's about Aleksander Kovac and his connection to your father."

David looked a little unnerved but soon regained his composure.

"Come in," he said, calmly.

David glanced quickly at the street to check that no one had noticed his visitors' arrival, before closing the door.

"This way please."

Max noted that the interior of the house hadn't changed much. David ushered Deanna and Max into an elegant sitting room, where two tall bookcases flanked an ornate fireplace. Large French doors overlooked a beautiful garden. David went over to the drinks cabinet, on top of which stood a collection of bottles, some glasses, and an ice bucket, as well as a phone. He then poured himself a glass of what looked like whisky.

"So what's this all about?" David asked, taking a sip from his drink.

"You don't remember me, do you, David?"

Deanna asked him.

"No, don't think so. Should I?"

"Well, it was twenty years ago," Deanna admitted. "You woke up on my couch and I brought you home."

"I'm sorry, I don't recall."

"I had green hair back then."

David suddenly looked very alarmed.

"What is this?" he demanded, slamming his glass down on top of the drinks cabinet. "What the hell's going on here?"

"When your father was working for the government," Deanna began, "he was involved in an operation at the waterfront. Aleksander Kovac used to experiment on psychics and other people with highly developed mental abilities."

"I don't know what you're taking about," said David.

"Look," said Deanna, "I understand you're concerned about protecting your father's reputation and—"

"I'm calling the police," David interrupted her, reaching for the phone.

"You were there at the waterfront, weren't you?" said Max, knowing they had to convince him. "You saw what your dad was involved in."

"No, I . . ."

"Max, no!" said Deanna.

"It's the only way we're going to get through to him!" Max exclaimed. "David, you saw the lab where they hurt people, didn't you? Remember that?"

"No, I . . . I don't know," David stammered, "I mean . . . how do you know all this?"

Max looked over at Deanna. He knew he couldn't tell David the truth.

"It's not important right now," said Deanna, "but someone's coming here to kill you."

"Who?" David demanded. "Who's coming here?"

"His name's Kane," Max replied. "He wants revenge."

"Revenge for what?" said David. "This is ridiculous. I don't know what you two are trying to pull here, but I'm definitely calling the police."

He reached for the phone again, but suddenly the French window shattered.

"What the–"

"Kane!" Max exclaimed.

Kane stepped through the shattered door into the room. David first staggered backwards then fell to his knees, knocking the ice bucket and several bottles onto the carpet. David clutched at his temples and his nose started to bleed as Kane stared intently at him.

"Leave him alone!" Max shouted.

He grabbed one of the full liquor bottles from the floor. He rushed toward Kane, who lashed out with his fist. The heavy blow caught Max firmly on the side of the head and he was sent reeling over to the bookcase, which fell on top of him. Max was groggy but remained conscious as Kane turned back toward David, whose face was streaked with blood. Max wasn't even sure if David was still breathing.

"You'll have to get past me first, before you hurt either of them!" yelled Deanna.

"You?" Kane scoffed. "I remember you from back at the lab. You're no match for me."

He turned his attention away from David and focused firmly on Deanna. Unlike David, she didn't collapse under Kane's onslaught. She defiantly stood her ground on the opposite side of the room, as she and Kane stared intently at each other. Kane grinned, his facial scar becoming more gruesome, while Deanna's brow began to furrow and she looked to be in pain. A trickle of blood appeared first beneath her nose, then another began running from her left ear. Max desperately wanted to help her, but he was pinned under the bookcase and couldn't move.

Suddenly, Max's mind was flooded with images. He saw a young girl, who he recognized from the images at the lab as the young Deanna, running through a field then cradling a puppy in her arms. He watched Deanna playing with the same dog when it was older, before glimpses of Deanna's teenage and college years quickly flashed by.

Then Max was viewing scenes from someone else's life. The boy couldn't have been more than five or six years old, but even at that age, Kane's features were unmistakable. Max witnessed the incident when Kane had killed a boy when he'd been testing his powers, followed by other snapshots from Kane's childhood and adolescence. There were even images from the lab when Kane was working with Kovac and the others.

Random scenes from both Deanna's and Kane's lives over the previous years flashed across Max's mind at ever increasing speed. Then abruptly, the images ceased and Max was once again witnessing the battle in the sitting room.

"No!" Kane exclaimed. "It's not possible! It's . . ."

Now it was Kane's turn to drop to his knees. With what appeared to be a final effort from Deanna, he fell sideways onto the carpet and lay still. Max watched as Deanna rushed over to David. She quickly checked his neck for a pulse, before heading over to where Max lay under the bookcase.

"Max! Max, are you okay?"

She managed to lift the bookcase just enough to be able to ease Max out onto the carpet. Deanna's nose was bloodstained and there was a trail of blood running down her cheek. Her hair was drenched in sweat as well as a little blood.

"Yeah, I think so," said Max. "What did you do to him?"

"I beat him, that's about the best way I can describe it," Deanna replied.

"Is he dead?" Max asked her, as he sat up.

"No, but he could be out for a while."

"So what happened?"

"We were kind of locked together," said Deanna. "Canceling each other out, I think, to be honest. I'm not sure why I was able to beat him. He was so much more advanced than I was when we were younger. Maybe his powers got weaker over the years, while I was always enhancing mine. Plus, he was probably still half focused on you and David."

"David!" Max exclaimed. "Is he okay?"

"Yes, he seems to be," Deanna assured him. "He's alive anyway."

"I saw things," said Max, grabbing her hand.

"Saw things?"

"Things from your life and his, in my head," said Max, "right up to when Kane collapsed just now."

"That's unusual," Deanna admitted, "but hey, this whole thing's pretty screwed up, isn't it?"

They heard a groan and went over to where David was struggling to sit up.

"David, are you okay?" asked Deanna.

"I'm not sure," David mumbled, as he got to his feet. "I have a heck of a headache. Oh, my god!"

In a mirror on the wall, David caught a glimpse of the blood on his face.

"He, um, hit you with something," said Max, thinking quickly.

David steadied himself on the drinks cabinet as he wiped his face with a small towel.

"Who is this guy?" said David.

He looked over at Kane, who lay still on the carpet.

"Like we told you, someone wanting revenge," Deanna replied.

"But for what?" said David.

"It's all about your father's connection to Kovac," Deanna started to explain. "This guy was, er . . . well, what I mean to say is—"

"He was one of the people who were kidnapped and experimented on," said Max, interrupting her. "He found out that your dad had been involved and knew no one would ever believe him."

"Yes," said Deanna, following Max's lead, "so he wanted revenge on your dad, or rather the next best thing—you."

"But I had nothing to do with anything like that," said David.

"Yes, we know that," Deanna told him, "but there he is, in your house. You'd better phone the police."

"The police?" said David. "But if this guy's connected to Kovac's work, I mean, not that I'm saying my father was involved . . ."

"It's fine, David," Deanna assured him. "I understand that you want to protect your father's reputation, but you really need to contact the police."

"But how do I explain him?" said David.

"Could just be a break in?" Max suggested. "I mean, your family's pretty well known and you were just in the paper, plus it's a big house."

"Yes, that might work," said Deanna.

"But look at that blood," said David, pointing at the wound that Max had inflicted on Kane earlier that day. "What's that all about?"

"Not sure," Deanna replied. "Maybe from when he came through the French window?"

"You could say you hit him with a poker," said Max, gesturing over at the fireplace.

"Would they believe that?" David asked.

"Self-defense against an intruder?" said Deanna. "It's worth a shot, but we really need to be out of here before the police arrive."

"Yes," David agreed, "yes, that might be best. Look, I really appreciate, you know, everything."

"You're very welcome, David," Deanna replied.

"Will we stay in touch?" asked David.

"It's probably best if we don't see each other again," Deanna advised. "This guy could talk to the police about some secret government experiment. Even if they think he's crazy, they could do some digging and find links to your dad. I think you'd want us to be well out of the picture."

"You're probably right," said David, shaking Deanna's hand. "Well, once again, thank you."

He then extended his hand to Max. When their palms met, Max's mind was once again flooded for a few seconds with David's memories. It seemed this time as if David had experienced something too.

"Are you sure we haven't met before?" he asked,

looking confused. "I mean, apart from at the cemetery? You seem so familiar somehow."

"We really do need to go, David," said Deanna. "And you need to call the police, before he starts to wake up."

Deanna and Max reached the front door and left the house, just as David began talking to the police.

"So, do you think the cops are going to buy it?" Max asked, as he and Deanna got into the car.

"No idea," said Deanna, "but it's better than trying to tell them the truth, don't you think?"

"But Kane's bound to talk."

"I'm not so sure about that," Deanna replied as they drove off. "You remember how he was able to almost fry people's brains when they doing those tests? I didn't mean to hurt him that badly, but the intensity of our mental fight may have burnt out some of his brain too."

"But he still might tell the police about Kovac and everything," said Max.

"Maybe," Deanna acknowledged, "but they might just see him as a rambling lunatic or someone with a grudge against David's father. Now, do you mind if we don't talk about this any more while I drive you home? I have one hell of a headache."

"So I really did change things," said Max as they drove into his neighbourhood "But I still don't understand. I mean, if David's still alive, how could I have met his ghost and gone back into his life?"

"I have to say," Deanna said, "that despite all my years of experience, I have no idea. It's incredible."

"And how come we still have memories from both

timelines?" asked Max.

"Again, I just don't know," Deanna replied. "And I have no idea how long these memories and thoughts will last either. You and I might always remember everything that's happened or we might not."

"But how can I just forget all this?"

"You may not have a choice," said Deanna as the car came to a halt outside Max's condo. "It could all just fade away. We might both wake up in the morning and not remember each other at all. Either way, I'm glad I was part of this."

"It wouldn't have happened without you," Max conceded. "Thanks for everything."

"You're welcome," Deanna replied, reaching across and giving his hand a squeeze. "Take care, Max."

"Hey Max," his dad called from the kitchen as Max opened the front door.

"Hi Dad," Max replied.

He saw the poker on the carpet in front of the fireplace and hoped that his dad wouldn't ask any awkward questions.

"So where've you been?" his dad asked, when Max reached the kitchen.

"Just out with friends," said Max, which was more or less the truth.

"Forgot to lock up earlier, didn't you?"

"Oh yeah, sorry," Max replied.

Locking the door had been the last thing on his mind when he was trying to escape from Kane.

"I must have just forgotten."

"Not to worry," his dad told him, with a smile.

"Hey look, I've been thinking. Why don't we take that trip?"

"What trip?"

"The fishing trip we keep putting off because I'm always so busy," his dad replied.

"Really?"

"Yeah," his dad continued, "I figured we've been putting it off for long enough. So what do you say? We could head out to the lake, maybe make a week of it?"

"That's great," said Max. "I didn't think we'd ever get to the lake, what with you working all the time."

Two weeks later, Max and his dad finally headed out on their fishing trip. Despite what Deanna had said, Max clearly remembered everything, both in the present and the past. He'd contemplated going to see Deanna, but in the end had decided against it. He was never going to forget what had happened, but wanted to put it all behind him.

Yet, as he sat beside the lake in the summer sunshine, Max knew he'd put things right.

BIOGRAPHY

Simon was born in Derbyshire, England and has lived in Calgary since 1990.

He is the author of *The Alchemist's Portrait*, *The Sorcerer's Letterbox*, *The Clone Conspiracy*, *The Emerald Curse*, *The Heretic's Tomb*, *The Doomsday Mask*, *The Time Camera*, and *The Sphere of Septimus*. Simon is also the author of *The Children's Writer's Guide*, a contributor to *The Complete Guide to Writing Science Fiction Volume One*, and has written many nonfiction books for younger readers.

Simon offers programs for schools, is an instructor with the University of Calgary and Mount Royal University and offers services for writers, including editing, writing workshops and coaching, plus copywriting for the business community.